# FRATERNITY

# FRATERNITY

## STORIES

## BENJAMIN NUGENT

FARRAR, STRAUS AND GIROUX

NEW YORK

Farrar, Straus and Giroux
120 Broadway, New York 10271

Some of these stories previously appeared, in different form, in the following
publications: *The Paris Review* ("God," "The Treasurer," and "Safe Spaces"); *VICE*
("Hell" and "Fan Fiction"); *Tin House* ("Ollie the Owl"); *The Best American Short
Stories* and *The Unprofessionals: New American Writing from The Paris Review*
("God"); and *The Best American Nonrequired Reading* ("Hell").

Library of Congress Control Number: 2020934843
ISBN: 978-0-374-15860-6

*Designed by Gretchen Achilles*

Our books may be purchased in bulk for promotional, educational,
or business use. Please contact your local bookseller or the Macmillan
Corporate and Premium Sales Department at 1-800-221-7945, extension 5442,
or by e-mail at MacmillanSpecialMarkets@macmillan.com.

www.fsgbooks.com
www.twitter.com/fsgbooks • www.facebook.com/fsgbooks

1   3   5   7   9   10   8   6   4   2

FOR EMILY

# CONTENTS

# GOD

We called her God because she wrote a poem about how Caleb Newton ejaculated prematurely the night she slept with him, and because she shared the poem with her friends.

Caleb was the president of our fraternity. When he worked our booth in the dining commons he fund-raised a hundred dollars in an hour. He had the plaintive eyes and button nose of a child in a life insurance commercial, the carriage of an armored soldier. He was not the most massive brother, but he was the most a man, the one who neither played video games nor rejoiced at videos in which people were injured. His inclination to help other brothers write papers and refine workouts bespoke a capacity for fatherhood. I had seen his genitals, in the locker room after lacrosse, and they reminded me of a Volvo sedan in that they were unspectacular but shaped so as to imply solidity and soundness. One morning when we were all writhing on the couches, hungover, he emerged from the bathroom in a towel, attended by a cloud of steam. We agreed that the sight of his body alleviated our symptoms.

"If you use a towel right after Newton uses it, your life expectancy is extended ten years," said Stacks Animal.

"If a man kisses Newton, he'll turn into a beautiful woman,"

I said, and everyone stared at me, because it was a too-imaginative joke.

But Newton threw his head back and laughed. "You guys are fucking funny," he said. "That's why I don't feel hungover anymore."

The putative reasons we named him Nutella were that it sounded like Newton and that he was sweet. But I wondered if it was really because when you tasted Nutella you were there. You were not looking at yourself from afar.

Nutella was never angry. When we discovered the poem and declared its author God, we knew he wouldn't object. He understood that it was a compliment to him as much as to the poet. To make Nutella lose at something, to deprive Nutella of control, God was what you had to be.

We learned of the poem's existence from Shmashcock's girlfriend, who was roommates with Melanie. (That was God's real name.) She told Shmash what the poem was about, and when she went to the bathroom he took a picture of it, and though it was untitled, he mass-texted it to us with the caption *On the Premature Ejaculation of Current Delta Zeta Chi Chapter President Caleb Newton.*

It was the only poem I'd ever liked that didn't rhyme. I read it so many times that I memorized it by accident:

> *Who is this soldier who did not hold his fire*
> *When the whites of my eyes were shrouded*
> *In fluttering eyelids?*
> *I thought I knew you*
> *Knew you were the steady hand on the wheel*

*The prow itself*
*But what kind of captain are you?*
*Scared sailor with your hand on your mast*
*Betrayed by your own body*
*As we are all betrayed*
*On your knees*
*Above me*
*Begging my forgiveness*
*With the muscles of a demon*
*And the whites of your eyes*
*As white as a child's?*

Behind the counter at D'Angelo/Pizza Hut, I whispered, "With the muscles of a demon / And the whites of your eyes / As white as a child's" for twenty minutes because it was the perfect description of Nutella. It was as if somebody had snapped a photo of him and enlarged it until it was the very wallpaper of my mind. I loved Melanie for writing it. I also felt I was her secret collaborator, for in my head I was contributing lines. I added:

*Whose hands are these?*
*One moment swift as a gray river*
*The next as still as stones*

Because that was another thing about Nutella. He was a war elephant on the lacrosse field and yet capable of quietude and stillness, reading econ on the porch, his phone facedown on his knee, casting light on his groin when he received a text.

5

While I refined my supplement to the poem, I prepared a Santa Fe Veggie Wrap. The process demanded that I empty a plastic bag of frozen vegetables into a small plastic bucket and place the bucket in a microwave. I neglected the microwave step and emptied the bag of vegetables directly onto the wrap, with the vegetables still cold and rigid. I realized what I had done when I laid the sandwich in its basket, presented it to the girl who had ordered it, and saw the gleam of frost on a carrot rod.

Evgeny called me into the management room, which was a yellow closet straining to contain Evgeny. He said that if I kept dreaming my days away I would wind up like him, a lover of art and philosophy. He pointed to his face, with its little black mustache. I promised him that from now on my motto would be No more spacing.

I took a pizza order and thought of all I was doing to enhance my employment prospects. Majoring in business, minoring in math, seeking internships related to data mining, building networks of contacts through Delta Zeta Chi, Campus Republicans, and Future Business Leaders. I dreamed of a consulting firm that Nutella would one day helm, staffed by brothers, known for underpromising and overdelivering, with an insignia depicting a clockface in the talons of an eagle. This would represent efficiency and superior perception. It would be pinned on each brother upon attainment of the status of partner, by Nutella, with live chamber music in an acoustically flawless atrium of recycled glass.

When the pizza emerged on the other side of the self-timing oven, I saw that I had neglected to sprinkle on the cheese. I used American slices intended for subs, room temperature, in the hope that they would melt on the freshly heated pizza in the course of delivery.

That night, Shmash read the poem aloud in the living room as Nutella covered his face and grinned.

"Like you all have never detonated early," he said, as if it was a dashing crime. As if this thing that we had all most likely done, and been ashamed of, was the least shameful thing in the world. I felt that all the brothers would have stormed North Korea for Nutella then, with a battering ram of wood and stone.

"That girl is a god," said Buckhunter.

"No," said Five-Hour. "That girl is God." And that was how it started.

We spied her at the dining commons the next day at lunch, by the tray carousel.

"God," shouted Five-Hour, and then we all shouted it.

She stopped and squinted. Her friends took up defensive positions on her flanks.

Shmashcock moved his arms up and down. "You are God for writing that poem," he said.

"God," we all said, and moved our arms.

She looked at Nutella, who was smiling.

"Yeah, that's me," she said. She kicked at Stacks, who was on his knees. "I guess you guys can worship me."

That night she came to the house with Nutella to hang out with us. I didn't know the nomenclature for her clothing. She wore black tights that went on her arms, green tights that came up to her knees, and a headband with tiny teeth that made the hair that passed through it poofy when it emerged on the other side. A wrist tattoo peeked from the lace at the end of her left arm tight. It was a picture of an old mill, a rectangular brick building. It represented Lowell, she said.

"The Venice of Massachusetts," said Buckhunter. His tone was that of an Englishman in a paisley monogrammed dressing gown, smoking a pipe.

"It's got canals," she agreed. Buckhunter cracked his knuckles and made an assertive sniffing sound.

What people often failed to realize about Delta Zeta Chi was that we were like Native Americans, in that our names referred to aspects of our personalities. Buckhunter was so named because in matters of girls he had the opposite of ADD. If a girl wandered within a certain radius of Buck, she robbed him of his faculty for reason. He couldn't assess her reactions to the things he said; he couldn't see or hear her clearly. He wanted it so bad he never got it. That was his tragedy, to be cockblocked by his own erect cock.

Like many girls before her, God said ha ha to Buckhunter, smiled disingenuously. I got her a beer and asked her questions. My name was Oprah because there were books in my room and I asked questions.

She wanted to work in public relations, she disclosed. She liked the Batman movies but not the X-Men movies. She was into Nutella as a friend.

God and Nutella made sandwiches in our kitchen. They were like two old men who had been in a war, or in a drag-out fight that neither had won. The poem, I supposed, had scoured away all pretense. Whereas the other girls who'd hooked up with Nutella, the ones who wanted him after the hookup and tried to date him, he treated with politeness and indifference. They were undead bumping their foreheads against our windows. They were the opposite of God.

After God and Nutella ate the sandwiches, they made carrot-ginger cupcakes for our midpoint-between-spring-break-and-summer party. In the course of so doing, they killed many ants in the kitchen and the velvety reef of mold in the sink. I offered to help with the cream cheese frosting because I was a frosting intellectual. Nutella argued with God about welfare entitlements versus the free market as he held a mixing bowl steady and she washed it with the rough side of a sponge.

That night God gave Nutella a spot while he did a keg stand, holding his calves above her head, her arm tights, now Easter-egg blue, taut against her forearms. God, we shouted. There were girls at the party so hot, their cheekbones so sharp, their heels so architecturally adventurous, their eyelids so thick with dark paste, they might have been the focus of male attention at a mansion with an in-ground pool. But these girls were not encircled by the brothers of our white ramshackle house. Only God was encircled.

We took turns dancing with her until Shmash asked if she wanted a beer. She declined, pivoted her way across the dance floor to Five-Hour, and humped the air near his leg. She said something in Five's ear and he said something back, and soon they were multitasking, their heads stabilized to enable conversation, their lower bodies humping on, like the abdomens of dying wasps.

Five and God went upstairs, Five leading the way, and we all watched Nutella. He threw his arms around me and Shmash and Stacks, and the blond hairs on his forearms were short and dry. His elbow slid around my neck and it was like rolling on a fresh-mowed August lawn.

"I want you guys to know," said Nutella, "that everything is completely cool. Five is the best man for the mission."

We did three Delta Zeta Chi owl hoots, and the sound was soft and Celtic against the human grunts and synthesizer belches of the music, and I wished the final owl hoot would never fade, our eight arms seized up forever around our heads, our huddle rotating slowly, as all huddles do, the faces of my brothers spinning in the black light. I remembered the day my mother took me to the Boston planetarium when I was seven, how the constellations maypoled around a void.


I always woke up earlier than anyone else in the house the morning after a party because I was protective of my abs and therefore drank less beer. That morning I descended to the kitchen to make breakfast and there was Five-Hour, with the shades pulled down and the song from last night's dance with God tinkling from his phone. He poured hard cider on his cereal.

"No matter what happened last night," I said, "some chocolate chip pancakes will taste better than that." I took the bottle from his hand and poured the cider and the cereal into the almost-full garbage bag sitting on the floor by the sink. I raised the shades. I mixed batter and chocolate chips.

"Help me," I said. "Slap some butter in a pan."

Soon there was the crackling and the smell.

"Big night?" I tried.

"Fuck you," said Five, "if you ever tell anyone else what I'm about to tell you went down."

I told him I wouldn't as long as he held the bowl so I could scoop the batter right. And he talked.

Once they were upstairs, he said, God had asked him please not to call her God and to call her Melanie instead. She hooked her phone to his speakers and asked him to take down the Eskimo-themed poster from the swimsuit issue. In all of this he obliged. When he tried to slide off her arm tights with his teeth, she said, "Funny not sexy," which threw him a little. Once her bra was off, she put a yarn-shop Simon and Garfunkel song on repeat and kissed him on the lips.

It occurred to him that this girl had been Nutella's breaker. Bedding her was, for a Delta Zeta Chi brother, what bedding Shania Twain would be for a Southerner or what bedding Natalie Portman would be for a Jewish person; he was belly to belly with the most major figure in the Delta Zeta Chi culture.

He thought of how Nutella, the least spastic person in the world, a man who could take a jab to the mask in lacrosse and not flinch, had burst open from her hotness, and how that explosion had been documented in a poem that was known to all our house, if not to all Greek houses. He, Five-Hour, was a champion of knights brought in to rescue a princess from a tower the king had failed to scale. I am SWAT, he thought, I am Lancelot. The more he considered it—how God was the ultimate princess, and he, therefore, the ultimate prince, deep in a forest impenetrable to others—the smaller and softer his dick became. For he could not believe that a supra-Nutellian knight was who he really was.

By this point in the telling, Shmash was loitering in the doorway of the kitchen, presumably drawn by the smell of batter. When Five and I looked up he retreated to the living room.

Five staggered to the corner of the kitchen and pressed his forehead against the wall. I turned off the stove and pinched his cheek. His face was wet. I have never cried—not once—since I was ten, and I admire people who can do it. The criers can see the admiration in my face, and it helps them talk.

"Do I just lie?" Five whispered. "Do I just act as if I fucked her, and if someone asks, say a gentleman never tells?"

I told him to tell the truth. To act like it was nothing to apologize for, because it wasn't. He fist-bumped me, weakly at first, but again and again, until the bumps acquired force. It was not what I had said, I think, because my advice was unremarkable. It was only that he could see the respect on my face, the respect for his tears, and respect, above all, was what he needed.

"I'm done telling Oprah about not getting it up last night," he called to the living room. "And he made pancakes."

Five minutes later everyone was in the sunny kitchen eating, brewing coffee, rinsing dirty plates, taking out the trash, crushing beer cans, talking about internships. Nutella squeezed fresh OJ wearing only his Red Sox boxers and baseball cap, and juice ran down his arms. Buck proposed a toast to Five for continuing the Delta Zeta Chi tradition of almost fucking God. Dust motes frolicked in the air as if emitted by our muscles, and the kitchen smelled like garbage, chocolate, sweat, and spring. I wondered if there would come a day when I would cry.

That night I had a dream I didn't want to have. In a white hotel room, I said to Nutella, *Why not? What's the reason for us not to, you and I? What harm?* I woke up spattered in cum and consoled myself as I washed my abs, hunched over the sink in the bathroom down the hall, with a different question: When thirty sportsmen slept beneath a common roof, the smells of their sweat joined in a common cloud, who could escape unsportsmanlike dreams?

The following evening was Otter Night at Theta Nu. We walked to the TN house with flattened cardboard boxes under our arms. To otter, you needed a cardboard box and a wet carpeted staircase. The theme of ottering was, look how brothers will pour buckets of water on a carpeted staircase, sled the stairs face-first, and be injured.

We ottered once a year at Theta Nu, but this Otter Night was remarkable for the presence of God, who'd been invited by Nutella. As soon as she climbed the stairs with the flattened box in her hand, we gave it up. None of us had seen a girl otter. To otter was to engage in a dick-bashing test of will. (Jockstraps were expressly forbidden.) To otter with tits was beyond imagining.

She stood at the top of the stairs, eyes closed, back straight. We shouted, drank, whispered that a girl wouldn't do it, filmed with our phones. She laid her box on the floor, looked at the ceiling above her, as if to consult a watchful parent. And then, to the ticking of a drum machine and the groans of a rapper and the groans of the rapper's woman floating above the rapper and the machine, she dove.

Her eyes flinched open every step. It was all quiet the three, four seconds of actual otter, but for the damp thump-*thumps* and a collective fraternal gasp. At the end, she reached for the banister to slow herself, a good move, and her landing at the bottom did not look unbearable. She came to a halt with her upper body on the soaked floor, her legs sprawled on the soaked stairs, her face in carpet, the cardboard sled tucked like a lover beneath her pummeled breasts.

"Give me a beer," she said, and I hugged Stacks, Nutella, and Shmash, and they hugged me back, and we all screamed, God, God, God.

Throughout the night, God drank beer and touched guys' arms. And a weird thing happened: the brothers declined to put the moves on her. No one steered her to the dance floor and freaked her. No one hovered beside her and asked her questions about her classes, holding his beer at chest height like a mantis to display his biceps.

The brothers were scared. Attempting her, Nutella had blown his load. Attempting her, Five had limp-dicked. And she ottered like a warrior. But to me she was a secret collaborator. We were both Nutella poets, the way people we read for our lit requirement were nature poets. I wasn't scared of her at all.

When the music went *Biggie Biggie Biggie*, I took her by the elbow and we took the floor. We humped the air between us; we collaborated. When the two of us left early, hand in hand, stumbling down Greek Row to Delta Zeta Chi, she said, "I have to say, I'm surprised this is happening with you."

I asked her what she meant.

"Just a wrong first impression."

The house was abandoned, all the brothers at TN's post-otter party, hoping to show off their injuries to girls who had seen them be brave. Our feet creaked on the stairs as she followed me up. In my room I gave her the plug to hook her phone to my speakers and asked her to choose music. She filled the room with the yarn-shopness that Five had described, and I recited her poem from memory, with the lines I'd added, while she sat on my bed with her chin on her fist.

"Consider it your poem, too," she said, and I knew I was supposed to kiss her, and I did.

I had never been to Silicon Valley, but that was where I went that night. Green grass in the shadow of silicon mountains, steel gray with chalk-white caps. Silicon wolves stalked the foothills, screen-eyed. I saw myself kneeling in that grass, doing for Nutella what God was doing for me. I made the sounds I thought Nutella would make.

I put on a condom as the yarn-shop song started over. When we were about to start fucking, I asked her to recite the poem. She looked at me for a moment. Please, I said, and she recited. I recited with her, and it worked: When we fucked, Nutella was close, because we had drawn him into the room like we were two lungs. He was just out of reach, something sprayed in the air, like a poem.

I only saw the blood when we were finished. I looked at her face for an answer. She sat and sucked air through her nose, wiped her face with the back of her hand.

"Were you thinking about Nutella?" she asked.

I said no in a too-deep voice.

"You're lying to me. Why did you want us to say the poem?" She started to cry. Her shoulders jumped in rhythm to her sobs. "It's cool, but at least don't lie to me."

Cry, I ordered myself. We would cry together. I pictured tide pools in my eyes. I pictured what the funeral would look like if my little sister died, her friends crying in their glasses and braces. But I'd tried to make myself cry many times, and always the same thing happened: my eyes knew I was trying to do it, and refused. I couldn't make myself cry any better than Nutella and Five-Hour could make themselves Melanie's lovers.

I waited for a minute, listening, trying to join. Finally, I leaned over and put my lips under her eye, so that I could taste her. I wanted to tell her what I tasted: sour makeup and salt.

"I'm sorry I lied to you," I said. "I thought about Nutella but also you at the same time." She took my hands and folded them across her ribs. And then something occurred to me.

"You can't write a poem about how I said that," I said. "About anything to do with me and Nutella. Even though it was your first time, you can't write a poem about it that you show to people."

I watched her blink in the dark.

"I might not write a poem about it," she said. "But I'm going to talk about it with my friends."

"You can't," I said. "You can't tell them I thought about Nutella."

"Okay, I won't," she said, and I knew that she was now the one lying.

I pulled away from her and sat up in bed. I could see what was going to happen to me like a film projected on my wall: My life was ruined. She would tell her friends, who would tell other girls, and Shmash or Five would find out from one girl or another. Shmash and Five would be too embarrassed to tell Nutella, but they wouldn't be able to resist telling other brothers, and one night, very drunk, a brother would tell Nutella. And nothing would happen. No one would say anything to me. No one would want to take anything from me. But brotherhood would be taken, in the end. The ease with which my brothers spoke to me, the readiness with which they spilled their guts in times of humiliation—this would be withdrawn. My place among them in the consulting firm of the clock and talons.

The atrium full of chamber music exploded, as if God had sung a note so high it shattered four stories of green windows.

I sat there hating her. She must have hated me back, because she got out of bed and put on her clothes without speaking. She had left the house by the time the brothers returned from TN. I lay awake and listened to them bang around the kitchen. They chanted in unison, a single, iambic owl: uh-*ooh* uh-*ooh*. It sounded like *beware, beware.*

# BASICS

t was the pregame for Eighties Tuesday, and most of the Kappas had come over to Delta house. It was dark outside, and in the living room the light was dim and the air was full of perfume. Zach arrived late because he'd been upstairs, lying on his bed, talking with his mother on the phone about whether or not he should buy an electric toothbrush. He took the last available seat, next to Sharon. Their only two previous conversations had revolved around professional basketball. The couch they shared was low and white, and she played with a tuft of stuffing that protruded from a tear in one of its arms. The volume on the TV was set so low that smaller explosions were inaudible. He sipped pale beer from a plastic cup.

She asked him if he liked the show. He shrugged. He didn't like superheroes anymore, he said. He didn't know what had changed. He'd been in love with superheroes when he was a child. He wasn't gay anymore, he explained, but he had been gay when he was little, if he thought about it. It was something about the briefs that the men wore over their tights. They were a different color from the rest of their costumes, so they drew the eye. And their pectorals were so much like breasts that they'd seemed to him a race of hermaphrodites, though he hadn't known the word. To be a superhero was to have parts from both sexes. That was how it had seemed.

As he spoke she drank hard cider from a narrow can she'd brought with her from Kappa. She peeled off its label in strips. She laid the strips on the arm of the couch and pressed them into the fabric with her pointer finger. She said that she, too, had been a gay child. Her first loves had been older girls, the assistant teachers in second grade. She still remembered their names: Sandra, Maura, Pauline. She hadn't regarded them as grown-ups, because they'd looked so much younger than her mother, and their hair had been so much longer. It was as if, when she was seven, girls her own age were human, and women were human, but older girls belonged to a higher species. They glowed. She had now reached the age at which little girls fell in love with her. She saw them look her up and down. When she had looked at older girls that way, as a child, what she'd wanted was to run away with them. In her fantasies, she said, one of them would take her by the hand and run with her through the lawns of her suburb. The two of them would help each other scale the fences and stone walls. Finally, when they reached a field, they would gather momentum, leap into the air, and fly, abandoning their families.

As she said this her face took on a sleepy expression. He couldn't tell to what degree they had discovered a special ability to be candid with each other and to what degree they were both already a bit drunk. Usually, at this point in a conversation with a girl, his throat constricted, his voice squeaked, he knocked things over with his elbow in the simple act of picking up a beer, and nothing he said sounded true. He asked her if she wanted to go up to the study room, where there was a large can of IPA from a Worcester-area microbrewery stowed on a shelf in a cardboard box that'd once contained a coffee maker. He explained that he kept it there so that his roommate wouldn't drink it. It was much better than the beer down here. She nodded. They stood and snaked their way through the couches.

In the study room upstairs, they sat on opposite sides of a desk, passing the tallboy. Retired oars hung from the wall, their shafts chewed by oarlocks, their blades painted purple and yellow. The overhead light flickered. The pregame was a faint noise beneath their feet.

He asked her if she thought she would still find the assistant teachers attractive, if she met them today. She said she didn't feel that way about individual women very often anymore. It was more like, sometimes, she had the desire to be an evil man, a CEO in a pin-striped suit who slept with his secretaries. She blinked at the floor and drank, self-conscious. We can't pause too long, he thought. He had to confess something immediately, to reciprocate her confession, or the exchange would grind to a halt.

It was the same with him, he said, in that he didn't desire particular men so much as think it would be cool to be an evil woman. He never dreamed of being a good woman, or a normal-looking woman, or a woman of average uprightness. He only realized that this was the case as he said it. He only dreamed of being a woman who was super fucked up and off-the-charts good-looking. He thought about long, dark hair piled on a pillow in a hotel room, mirrors with brass stuff on the frames. He could imagine fucking rich morons. He couldn't imagine being a woman with a good man, a man who had loftier aims than making money, who lived according to principles. That sounded like a nightmare.

Sharon sipped the ale, handed it back to him, and said, "We're both evil." She narrowed her eyes and slouched, like a crone, and pointed her finger at him. "You, too, are an evil one." She said it in a crone's hoarse voice. She made her finger tremble, to give the crone a parkinsonian ailment. "It's true that you have kind of an evil face," she continued, returning to her normal way of speaking, but doubling down on the crone's posture, leaning even farther across the desk. "I don't like it. I want to slap it." She raised one hand as if to swat his cheek but she didn't do it.

They could hear the pregame draw to a close. People whooped with excitement at the prospect of marching through the cold to the Hangar and dancing on a floor with shifting patterns. In anticipation of Eighties Tuesday, someone had put on a song from the eighties. *You were working as a waitress in a cocktail bar*, the man sang, and the lyrics that followed were indecipherable. Zach knew that his brothers were lacing their brogues and sneakers. He knew that Sharon's sisters were pulling on their heels. This was the last chance to go downstairs and join them. They sat and listened to the departure.

He went to his room to find his roommate's cigarettes. They smoked on the porch. They stood barefoot in the inch of snow on the grass, to see how long they could bear it. She said his cologne was so strong that standing next to him was a greater test of endurance than standing in the snow. She said it was like he was a dying Abercrombie store trying to attract customers with its smell. For the first time in his life, he genuinely wanted to dance with a person. He almost suggested they join the others at the Hangar for Eighties Tuesday, but he was worried that his dancing would depress and embarrass them.

Instead he worked up his courage and told her she could slap him in the face if she did in fact want to. He blushed, surprised at how much this sounded like an offer to have sex. He felt like a cat that had turned around and raised its hindquarters in the air. She bit her lip, struggling with a decision.

"Okay," she finally said, with some ambivalence. "Yeah. I'll slap you."

"Cool," he said. They decided to go inside first, and stood facing each other in the living room, warming their feet on the carpet, drinking the last of the beer from the keg.

"I'd feel more comfortable," she said, "if we both hit each other. You can hit me in the stomach. It's actually strong. I don't know why."

It was; she took his hand and pressed his palm to her belly, to show him. She never did any sit-ups, she said, it had something to do with her genes. He agreed that he would hit her in the stomach, but he said that he thought she should hit him in the face first, since she was the one who had brought up the idea of hitting, by saying she wanted to slap him. She nodded and grazed his face with the tips of her fingers.

"Sorry," she said, "that was terrible." He told her not to worry, that it was okay. They were both standing behind the white couch on which they'd sat earlier that evening. A small amount of her beer had spilled on the floor when she'd slapped him unsuccessfully. She really should have put down her beer first, she said. That was one of the reasons she'd slapped him so clumsily. Once she had placed the cup by her feet she assumed a stance that she said she'd learned on her high school volleyball team: feet planted shoulder-width apart, low center of gravity. And then she hit him in the stomach, which surprised him, though it wasn't very hard. It was different from how it felt when he'd put on boxing gloves and sparred with other Deltas. He could feel the impact of her two front knuckles, each of them distinct and sharp.

"Why can't you hit me in the face," he asked her, "if you don't like my face?" He became conscious of his breathing. She had risen from her volleyball posture. She seemed to consider his question, her head tilted to one side. She looked out the window, at the snow that was being picked up by the wind, and back at him again, and nodded, as if to say, *Yes, there's a small amount of snow lifting off the ground.* And then they were lurching across the room as a single inelegant creature, kissing, knocking over cans, spilling beer and cider. The fizz of the spilled drinks on the carpet was a dirty sound. His eyes were closed but he could hear a truck slicing through the slush in the street, splashing cold water as it passed. There was traffic on North Pleasant. Someone was leaning on a car horn. Massachusetts was covered in snowdrifts that were stained by exhaust around the edges. Was this what people meant by "dirty," when they spoke of a mood that could descend on lovers, this feeling of being part and parcel of the world?

They looked at each other, their arms wrapped around each other's waists. They took the narrow back stairs that led to the third floor holding hands.

"I hate your room," she said, as she followed him in and shut the door. He said he hated his roommate's fridge. She said she hated that it had no beer inside. He said that he hated his rug, as he rubbed his feet against it, and it was an ugly rug, its pattern alternating squares of black and gray. His roommate had ordered it from Lowe's and they'd never had an honest conversation about it. It was like *Goodnight Moon*, the game of declaring their hatred for each object. He chose a playlist on his phone and connected his phone to his speakers. The music was unobtrusive, instrumental hip-hop, and now its very unobtrusiveness struck him as contemptible. "I hate this music," he said.

They climbed into his bed and undressed each other. She said that she hated men. Their hatred for all the things they'd mentioned was a kind of languor, a drug. He felt oddly inoculated against judgment, taking his clothes off in front of her. It was better to feel her hands on his skin and think, *She hates my skin*, than to think, *Does she love my skin?* It was better to feel her hands in his hair and think, *She hates my hair*, than to think, *Does she love my hair?* He could feel that he had become a better kisser than he usually was, because he wasn't as nervous.

They stopped talking while he fingered her. When she pulled his hand away, he took a condom from a drawer in his nightstand and put it on. She dragged him on top of her, and then they were having sex, slowly, wearing expressions of affected disdain. He was twenty-two years old, a senior in college, he'd had sex four times, and every time, he knew, he had been the worst lover in the world. He'd heard of men who lasted a minute spoken of as shitty in bed, but he couldn't fathom how any man had been able to last thirty seconds. A minute was herculean. All four times, a combination of panic, gratitude, and reverence had overwhelmed him within ten or fifteen seconds, or five. But now everything was different. It astonished him, the power of this new way of doing things, of doing things in a spirit of fake hostility. When he'd approached sex in a spirit of love, he'd felt like a rabbit, and now he felt like a sloth, in a good way. It seemed like a realistic possibility that he could go on doing it for a long time. Look at us, he thought, a couple of stupid little ugly dirtbags. He felt that he was hovering over the bed, watching two people at their work. They were both making the sounds people made on television. *Look at these two little assholes*, he thought, hoping to maintain the mood that had proven so helpful. It was incredible how slowly they were moving, how much time had passed, perhaps a minute already. This was what it was supposed to be like.

I am not being guided by intelligence, he thought, I am being guided by instinct. That's how it works if you know what you're doing. He pinned her arm to the bed beside her hair, and then, when she made an encouraging sound in response, he propped himself up on one elbow and—it felt like just another sound he made—put a hand on her throat and applied a small amount of pressure with his fingers.

Her face fell and went blank. This was the problem with the fake hostility, he saw: it was unclear how far it was supposed to go. Her face was still fallen after he took his hand off her neck, and he wondered if he should get off her and apologize. But it seemed wasteful to let everything go to hell. He thought, *We'll recover, we'll find our way back to how it was before*. He gazed into her eyes like a really nice person, as they continued to have sex.

He made the face of a gentle lover, dropping his mouth open. And these contrivances turned out to be another mistake, because she shook her head and looked away. A moment later, she told him to stop. This happened at the same time he realized that he might be about to come, and the confluence of the two events was so disorienting that he froze, as if "stop" were a demand for the cessation of all movement, rather than a demand for withdrawal. He lay on top of her, limp, breathing hard, his head resting beside hers on the pillow, for more than five seconds, less than ten, neither of them speaking, or moving, and then he came. It felt like a clerical error, like clicking send when you meant to click save. He pulled out and looked at her, and she was averting her eyes and covering them with her hands.

He sat beside her and tried to read her body language. She was lying on her side, turned away from him. He felt tenderness and regret. How was it possible he had hurt this person whom he was so intent on pleasing? And then the tenderness and regret were mingled with fear. What was it called, what had just happened? Was his hesitation in pulling out of her and getting off her when he knew he was about to come a form of aggression, for which he deserved punishment, or was it a brief stupor, a natural effect of having sex? She wasn't looking at him. She was looking at the wall.

"Sorry," he heard himself say. "I didn't mean to be too . . ." He knew that this was an unsatisfactory description of what he'd done, but he was afraid that he would use the wrong words if he tried again to describe it. He reached out and stroked her hair, until she jerked away. She said nothing, only searched under the blanket and sheets for her clothes.

He stopped talking and sat naked in bed, watching, as she extracted her underwear and socks from the bedding and started to dress.

"Are you okay?" he asked.

She turned to him and shrugged. She threw up her hands and shook her head. She didn't know if she was okay or not, she seemed to be saying, or at least she didn't know the degree to which she didn't feel okay. *Neither of us understands what just happened*, he thought. *Neither of us understands the nature or seriousness of what I've done wrong.* It seemed to him that there was a moment of accord, in which they each registered the other's confusion. And then she left.

As soon as he heard Sharon leave the house, he called his mother. He tried her cell and then her landline. She picked up on the fourth ring and asked him if he was okay. He could tell from the sound of her voice that he'd woken her up. He could see her standing in her bedroom in the house in Agawam, barelegged in a T-shirt. She had put on her glasses, he guessed, and now she was looking out the window at the snow caked on the neighbors' solar panels, the black driveways with sharp corners.

"I think I might have sexually assaulted someone," he said. "I don't know."

She told him that he didn't need to stop crying but that he did need to speak clearly and slowly, so that she could understand what he was saying. "Don't be shy," she said. "You need to tell me exactly what happened. Don't leave anything out."

He told her.

"Wait," she said, "go back. How long was it between when she said to stop and when you ejaculated in the condom, inside her?"

He tried to remember the precise length of time, counting one-Mississippi two-Mississippi in his head as he replayed the moment. He sniffed back mucus and tasted it on his tongue. "Like maybe six seconds," he said. "Maybe seven. But I'm not sure."

"And then you pulled out?"

"Yeah. She looked upset."

His mother laughed with relief. "From how you were talking about it," she said, "I'd have thought it was two minutes."

He waited for her to go on.

"Look," she said. "You may have to go to some kind of counseling. But you're not going to get expelled. If the university expelled all the guys who did what you did, they would lose a lot of money. If the cops charged all the guys who did what you did with a crime, a lot of people would have to go to jail."

He toppled backward onto the bed and stared at the ceiling. Everything looked beautiful and new now that she'd told him he was safe. The snow sparkled in the porch light. Despite the weather, a car drove by with its windows down and its stereo on, playing dance music.

"You need to be more careful," his mother said. She made a pained sound. "Did she seem like she was going to be okay?"

He touched the sheets where Sharon had lain naked less than ten minutes earlier. He skimmed his hand back and forth across them, still holding the phone to his ear. "Should I go to Kappa and apologize?"

There was a long silence. His palpitations came and went. He heard her fill a glass with water at the kitchen sink. Or maybe she was filling a kettle for tea.

"Well," she said, "of course you should be nice to her, but let's give everyone a chance to calm down. If you tell her you're sorry, in an emotional way, like something really serious happened, she might decide that something really serious happened. Everyone's tired and worked up. Let's talk tomorrow, before you think about saying anything." She spoke to him of the riskiness of all intercourse, of the possibility of unwanted pregnancy, of catching diseases. She reminded him of the importance of listening carefully to girls and paying close attention to their signals. These were things she'd told him many times, and he found it soothing to hear them again, like a storybook from childhood.

"I'm sorry," he said intermittently, as she spoke to him.

"You don't need to apologize to me," she said, but he continued to do so, whenever there was a pause in the conversation. After a while, his breathing slowed and he almost felt capable of sleep.

But he didn't sleep after he got off the phone. He went downstairs to clean up the mess he'd made with Sharon. The floor of the living room was littered with bottles and cans that they'd knocked off the arms of chairs and couches. He'd never cleaned a floor before, so he didn't know whether to use the broom or the mop, or, if he was supposed to use them both, which came first. The carpet had absorbed most of the spilled beer, so he went with the broom. Only one of the bottles had actually shattered. He tried to sweep the shards into a little pile, but some of them were lodged in the fabric.

He was on his knees, picking out the glass with his hands, when the front door swung open. Four Deltas had come home early from the Hangar, led by Five-Hour, who was singing the song that had been playing toward the end of the pregame: *"I was working as a waitress in a cocktail bar / That much is true."*

He didn't want to talk to Five-Hour, so he looked away and returned to his task.

"What are you doing?" Five-Hour asked. "Why are you cleaning at night?"

He dropped the last of the shards into his cupped palm and went to the kitchen to throw the mess in the trash.

"Did something happen?" Five-Hour asked, following him.

He could see the others settling on the floor by the TV in the living room and resuming a PS4 game they'd paused in the afternoon. He heard the clatter of hooves and remembered there'd been talk of a cavalry engagement. There was an exchange of fire, repeater carbines in a valley or ravine, and then there were the cries of shot horses. How many guys our age, he wondered, have sat together at night, during a war, and listened to the sound of horses dying?

He sat with Five-Hour in the kitchen and told him what he'd done. He told him about the talk he'd had with his mother. "I see," Five-Hour said.

He asked Five-Hour if he should try to talk to Sharon. Five-Hour dug in his backpack and took out a box of red licorice.

"If you think about it," said Five-Hour, chewing on a lump,

"you don't want to roll up to her and start talking if she's not initiating it. That might make it worse."

He shook his head, though he didn't know why he was objecting to Five-Hour's advice. And then he said something he hadn't known to be true until he said it, which was that he couldn't help but feel everything had gone wrong precisely because he and Sharon had hit it off. The thing that had happened had happened not because they didn't care about each other, or didn't like each other, but because they did care about each other and did like each other. That was why things had moved so fast and the whole thing had spun out of control. It was like how a sports car with an amazing engine was more likely to crash into a wall than was a minivan with a shitty engine. "Fuck it," he said, "I'll just message her," and picked up his phone. There was a closed Greek Facebook group to which everyone in Delta and Kappa belonged, so she was probably in his Messenger contacts.

He'd barely touched the screen when Five-Hour slapped the phone out of his hand. It hit the floor some distance from the table where they sat, its rubber case causing it to bounce slightly on the linoleum.

"My brother," said Five-Hour, "you raped her, a little bit." He threw up his hands. "In the eyes of the school, for however many seconds, that's what you did." They'd all been taught the affirmative-consent policy in first-year orientation, he pointed out. Even now, he said, she might be talking to her friends in Kappa, trying to decide what to do. Would people believe her— that would be her problem, if she wanted to start a J-Board. All she needed was a DM from him saying *Sorry, I fucked up tonight,* and problem solved. "Turn off the phone," said Five-Hour. "Go to sleep, and don't turn it on again until it's morning. Don't confess."

He woke hungover, his roommate snoring in the bed kitty-corner to his own. Pink sunlight had crept onto the snowy eaves of the house across the street. He put on jeans and a hoodie, went downstairs, and drank two glasses of water. To treat his headache with fresh air, he put on his coat and sneakers and went outside.

The snow was ankle-high and smooth, save for two sets of footprints created by bare feet. They ran down the slope of the yard, one slightly smaller than the other, and stopped at the arbitrary spot where he and Sharon had smoked his roommate's cigarettes and hopped up and down, shifting their weight from one foot to the other to keep their toes from going numb.

He walked downtown, past the other fraternities, to buy a coffee at the convenience store. The day was mild enough for a little of the snow to melt. Water pattered from tree branches onto the roofs of SUVs parked in driveways, and onto an empty beer can that lay crushed beside a bush.

At the corner of Fearing and North Pleasant, children were waiting for the school bus. There were three boys and two girls, the oldest maybe twelve, the youngest seven or eight. All of them wore down jackets with their hoods thrown back, their heads exposed. They had the disconsolate look of people barred from using phones. They muttered to themselves, stomped the ice, packed snowballs only to drop them on the ground. That little girl, he thought, is in love with the older girl. The older girl is thinking about what it would be like to be an evil man summoning his administrative assistant into his office after hours. The older boy is wondering what it would be like if he and the older girl were hermaphrodites in tights, who slept in a secluded mansion with others of their kind. The children were not having those thoughts—he couldn't know what they were thinking—but it was possible, even likely, that the thoughts they were having were equally unmentionable. The world was more interesting now that he and another person had been free with each other.

In the convenience store, he poured two thimblefuls of non-dairy creamer into his coffee. There was White Chocolate and Irish Crème, and today he went with Irish Crème. The creamer was revolting, but he wanted it, too. Was that what he had been like for her, last night, before things went wrong? That is, had she found him disgusting but also compelling? That was how it had seemed. It had been a new feeling, being liked and disliked in that way.

He took out his phone and opened the closed Facebook group. He wasn't one of Sharon's friends, so the pictures of her he could see were mostly shots of her whole pledge class as it advanced through the years. There was one photo of her with two other Kappas, sitting on a couch in the Kappa living room, stoned, pointing to their pink eyes. A bowl of guacamole was bathed in the blue light of the TV.

In addition to the coffee, he bought a spiral-bound notebook, a box of envelopes, and a pack of cigarettes. A bell jingled as the door slammed behind him and he came out into the cold. He sipped the coffee as he walked, spilling it down his coat. The sunlight was no longer pink. The buildings on either side of North Pleasant—a motel, a sports bar, a chain Italian restaurant—had ceased to be pretty and become their usual daylight selves. He watched a pair of joggers, a middle-aged couple with metal cleats strapped to the soles of their sneakers. Each of their footfalls splattered slush across the pavement. He wondered what Sharon thought of him, and whether she herself knew what she thought of him, as he descended the stairs to the mailroom on the edge of campus. He still didn't know if he deserved to be punished, or, if he did, how severe the punishment should be.

In the mailroom there was a small counter with a pen on a chain. He took an envelope out of the box he'd bought at the convenience store and tore a page from the notebook.

He wrote quickly. He said that he knew he'd done something wrong, and broken the rules, that he was sorry and hoped to improve the situation in some way. He signed his name and wrote his number beneath his signature. He dropped the note and cigarettes into the envelope, and hesitated. *I can still throw it out*, he thought. *I can still change my mind.*

It was desire, even more than shame, that made him lick the envelope, seal it, write her full name on the front, and hand it to the man behind the desk. He was afraid. But he wanted to talk to her again, and this was the only way to make it happen.

# FAN FICTION

lived in the basement of a split-level built on a hill. The carpet was pine green. There was no kitchen. I kept ready-made sandwiches from Trader Joe's in a brown minifridge, and the outline of a sandwich was embossed in burnt sauce on the microwave's plate.

I liked to go running in the empty park, where big crows watched from the trees as I passed. The dust was golden orange. It worked its way into the treads of my sneakers and from my sneakers into the carpet, so that when the sun shone through the basement windows, the green material sparkled here and there with desert hues.

Exercise was important to me. My brothers in Delta had often said, *Nutella's fairest of us all*, and I'd pretended not to be affected by their flattery. Now, when an audition had gone badly, or my agent had been slow to return one of my e-mails, I would put on music, take off my clothes, and look at myself in the mirror. At least I'd made my body. It wouldn't last forever. That was why I had to be here now, while I was young. This was the window. My body had brought me Carla, or, to be more exact, I don't think the two of us would have lasted an hour without it. I wouldn't have been able to act normal around her if I hadn't had a superpower of my own, however minor.

I never asked her for help with my career. When she wondered aloud if she should cast me in her next film, I said no, she had to follow her vision. We avoided bars where I couldn't afford to buy my own drinks. I paid for half of everything, except for twice, when we went to resorts she wanted to try, in Montana and Big Sur, and on my birthday, and every once in a while, when she wanted to sit at a table on a deck overlooking the ocean, and for me to be there with her.

At midprice restaurants, waitresses told Carla how much they'd loved her film. At expensive restaurants, the hostess would tell the manager she was there, and the manager would bring free appetizers. One manager, a plump bald man in a suit, laid out three bowls of lemon mousse and three spoons. He called for wine and three glasses. "It's been such a fucking night," he said to Carla as he sat down. We'd never met him before.

One afternoon, the weather was black snow, ash from a fire in the Inland Empire. Pedestrians on Echo Park Avenue turned up their palms to catch the flakes. It didn't happen where Carla lived, closer to the sea. "I'm jealous of your neighborhood," she said, when I told her about it.

One evening when I was taking a shower at Carla's house, she knocked on the bathroom door. When she drew back the curtain, the sound of the water changed.

"Show me your asshole," she said. I turned, bent my knees, drew apart my buttocks, and let them fall back in place. She giggled for a long time and said, "That is just so wonderful." I stayed longer in the shower than I had to, after it happened, while she sat on the toilet and read aloud from a novel I'd never heard of, a passage she hoped would move me. "You're a good boy," she said, as she shut the book. "I bet you never gave your mama any trouble." There was something about the water and the humiliation, heat on heat. It became a ritual. Whenever I took a shower, Carla would creep in on cat feet, draw back the curtain, and shout at me to show it. It never got old. I don't know why it made me so happy.

Our first three months were an extended fling. There was no talk of love. Whenever I try to describe how it became serious, the result is a series of clichés, so I'm going to let Carla take over. I'm going to imagine what the film would be like if she were to write and direct a film about what happened.

Caleb Newton, seven years ago a fraternity president, now a struggling actor, is on his knees in a weight room, doing military presses with chrome dumbbells that clank when he knocks them together above his head. His phone vibrates on the mat.

Behind the gym, in a cramped parking lot with cracks in the asphalt, and weeds in the cracks, their leaves wilted in the heat, he leans over the hood of a hatchback, his shirt stained with sweat, his cell phone to his ear, and listens to loud breathing on the other end of the line. Just tell me, he says. Why are you—

An eight-story office building in Century City, just off Wilshire Boulevard. It's early. There are scattered strips of purple cloud in a pink sky. A teal 1975 Lincoln, its white roof raised, descends a ramp into an underground garage.

Caleb at the stainless-steel steering wheel, guiding the wide car into a parking spot, his clothing casual and plain: jeans, a white T-shirt. Beside him in the passenger seat: Carla Dakopoulos, a film director, only two years his senior, but sought-after and acclaimed. She wears sweatpants, a hoodie, and a baseball cap.

We should put it on your card, she says. I'll pay you back. He kills the engine. No, he says, I'll—

A two-shot, from the back seat. We see the dashboard, and two heads of hair. No, she says, I'll reimburse you. But we should use your card. People get—I'm not going to tell them my name. It's better if the receptionists and the nurses don't know who—I'm not an actor so it probably won't happen, it's a thing that mostly happens to actors, but I still—they can threaten to sell the receipt or whatever to a tabloid. But—

A close-up of Caleb's hands tapping the wheel. Of course, we hear him say. Of course we'll put it on my card.

Decor in the reception area: red Chinese fans; a watercolor of a seaside cliff; a small sculpture of a cat in a bow tie.

A nurse in blue scrubs stands in a doorframe. Joanne? she says. Carla stands.

Carla no longer wears her baseball cap. She leans against the wall of an elevator and closes her eyes. Some of her hair is stuck to her face. She wipes her mouth with the back of her hand as she falls asleep. Caleb takes her by the shoulders and pulls her away from the elevator's wall.

A handheld shot, through the Lincoln's driver-side window, of passing billboards: VEEP, GEICO, IT'S TIME FOR DODGER BASEBALL IN 4:18:05, 4:18:04, 4:18:03.

Carla sleeps on a bed with white sheets, in a bedroom with gallery-white walls and large windows covered with gauzy curtains. She's curled up on her side. On the nightstand, there's a small framed drawing an artist gave her, a portrait of the two principal characters from her film. Caleb stands beside her bed and watches her. He takes the little sketch from the nightstand and holds it to the light.

The low desert at sunset, framed by the Lincoln's windshield. The roof is down. Carla, in the passenger seat of the rumbling car, lights a cigarette using the car's detachable lighter, her hair and the smoke whipped back by the wind.

I can hear Carla in my mind's ear: *I would never shoot a scene with a young couple smoking cigarettes in a vintage car headed to Twentynine Palms. I would gouge my eyes out before I put that in a film.*

And I say: *But that's what happened. That is the car you owned. You liked to smoke with the top down, and your feet on the dash, on a desert road. Because deep down you still loved that kind of movie, even though you were too smart to make that kind of movie. We love the things we think we've gotten over. It's nice to have you back in my head, directing.*

A coyote sniffs at the trunk of a Joshua tree. It looks at them.

That's him, says Carla. She points at the coyote.

I still think it might have been a girl, says Caleb, driving.

No, that's our baby, says Carla. That's the second coyote this week he's inhabited.

The car climbs a gentle slope toward a small cluster of windmills.

Close-up on a windmill's face, its three thin blades spinning slowly in the brown and violet evening. No child of mine is growing up to be a scavenger dog, we hear Caleb say. A coyote's a scavenger dog. He's not a scavenger, we hear Carla reply. He's figuring things out. He'll be okay.

■  ■  ■

Carla mostly worked behind the camera. So the fans who accosted her on the street were educated people. One of them told her she was quietly subversive. Another told her she was a throwback to the age of the auteur. When they looked at her, there was something in their faces that was rare and handsome: concentration.

Carla was beautiful when she humored fans. She liked to rummage in her bag for a Nat Sherman as they stood there watching her, produce one with a show of triumph, and ash on the heel of her hand. She became smaller and brighter. Her high school self, that big-nosed girl with flyaway curls, wouldn't stop haunting her, so she wore her power like a joke, smiled with her teeth, arms folded, eyes incredulous. I saw why some other famous people, other kinds of famous people, had entourages; I thought Carla might be happier if she always had some friends around to remind her that everyone loved her, that the high school Carla was never coming back.

Once, when we were waiting in line to buy hot dogs from a kiosk at the airport, a teenage girl was talking on her phone to her friend about her flight delays when she abruptly changed the topic of conversation.

"Wait. Stop. I'm standing behind Carla Dakopoulos at a hot dog stand," murmured the girl. "Yeah. She's talking to this guy about how he has to read this book she's carrying. I thought he was Thor, but he's not Thor. She's wearing white Converse and white nineties jeans and this red polka-dot top with one of those little belts in the back. Now she's ordering a hot dog. This is embarrassing, she's looking at me. You owe me. I'm embarrassed. Yes, right at me. Now she's turned away again."

■　▩　▩

The first e-mail from my ex-girlfriend came when I was watching an old French sci-fi film composed of still photographs. Carla had assigned it to me; she said it was Film 101. She had just left my apartment for a meeting in Universal City. The sharp, joyous smell of new tires hung in the air. This was the smell our vibrator released after it was cleaned.

> Nutella,
>
> Hope it's not weird to still call you that? Is it true you're dating Carla? She's one of our clients. How's that going? She's a lucky woman. I recently sold a documentary-style show on competitive gamers for frankly a lot more money than I thought I would. It made me think of your mom's boyfriend's computer game addiction.
>
> Hope you're well,
> Olive

The last time Olive and I had stood face-to-face, she'd said that it was so sad watching me decline from an ambitious fraternity president fresh out of college to a benumbed failure that she no longer ever truly wanted to sleep with me. "If you want," she'd said, "you can wait until I fall asleep and poke me. I understand you have needs."

It was odd that now she would keep me abreast of her accomplishments. I showed the e-mail to Carla that night, in the interest of transparency.

"She walks like a duck," Carla said. That was not right. When Olive wore heels, she threw her legs in front of her and swung her arms, as if she were worried about losing forward momentum.

"True," I said to Carla. "You always nail people. I guess because you're a director."

Carla scrambled off my mattress and duckwalked up and down the green carpet, smoking her cigarette, looking nothing like Olive.

"Oh my God—uncanny," I said, clapping. "Hi, Olive."

We had sex, building to the vibrator, and watched *The Lion King*. I wanted Carla to see it so that she could see the real America. Carla's father was a film scholar. Her mother directed an arts foundation. Carla had grown up in Brooklyn and learned to drive at twenty-seven.

Mufasa, the dad lion, was showing Simba, the child lion, the savanna over which he would one day reign. "Everything the light touches is our kingdom," Mufasa said.

"That's it," I said. "That's our country. That's what it's like. My dad once took me out for a drive, when he found out I had grown some pubic hair, and he was like, 'I want you to know you can have anything you want, son, if you go out and work for it.' And he let me hold the wheel, so I could see what it felt like to be a man." This was not true.

"That's so bad," she said. "That's kind of fucked." She laid her head on my shoulder. I think she knew I was lying. I think she knew I knew she knew I was lying. We had a tacit understanding: every once in a while, I got to be the artist, and she got to be the audience.

When the movie was over, she knelt on my mattress and looked out the window. My purple-and-yellow Delta Zeta Chi sweatshirt was all she wore. She liked the sweatshirt because it proved my world was real.

"The thing about the people in that movie," she said of *The Lion King*, "is that they're all struggling with real problems."

"Most people," I said, "have real problems."

"Of course." She shook her lighter, which, resting on the sill during the climax of the movie, had been exposed to light rain. "But they don't attack their real problems, typically. They attack fake problems while their real problems eat them alive. That's what good movies get that Disney movies don't."

"Before you respond to Olive's e-mail," she said, as we were falling asleep, "show me what you're going to say."

"Whatever you want," I told her, and fit two of her knuckles in my mouth.

▪    ▪    ▪

I was eating a late breakfast in a booth by myself at a coffee shop in Burbank. The walls were covered with autographed photos of actors. The pie case was taller even than its counterpart at

the House of Pies. I'd just finished my broccoli-egg-white om-
elet when I looked up and saw the manager standing over me,
his hands in a prayerful position, a busboy standing behind
him with a dish towel thrown over his shoulder.

"Sir," said the manager. "Excuse me, I'm so sorry to bother
you. But are you Tye Sheridan?"

I slugged down the rest of my coffee. In no sense was I Tye
Sheridan, or his near equivalent. I didn't even look like him.
I bore a stronger resemblance to the Hemsworths. What the
man had seen on me was professional skin, professional muscles, professional hair, and a face that would pop on camera, if
given a chance. "That's me," I said humbly.

"It's an honor to meet you," the manager said. We shook
hands. The busboy stepped forward and produced a clipping
from a magazine, Sheridan in *Ready Player One*. The manager
smoothed it out as he laid it on the table. I don't remember the
words he used when he asked for my signature and dedication.
What I remember is his helpless grin, and the helpless grin of
the busboy behind him, their submission.

■   ■   ■

The next morning, I showed Carla my proposed reply to Olive: *We're so in love. So cool that you sold the gamer show.* Carla
approved it and I tapped send. Thirteen minutes later, Olive
replied:

> *Carla D. and Nutella in love . . . adorable, and it should
> help with your acting.*

*I still remember how anxious you were about your career. You were so paranoid that nothing would ever work out for you and now look at you, dating a wunderkind. I think you are going to be huge, a legend. We'll all be looking at your face on billboards. Do you still not talk to your dad since he sent you the McKinsey internship application?*

I could feel that Carla was angry as she read it over my shoulder.

"She wants you back," she said. "She's big-upping you and negging you, now that you're dating me, because of my . . ." The omitted word was *fame.*

I agreed that Olive's interest in me had been revived by my dating a famous person. But she didn't want me back, I explained. She didn't want to sleep with me per se, she just wanted to share something with Carla. It could be me, a doula, anything of an intimate nature.

Carla was unmollified by my take on the situation. She was throwing on her blazer, looking for her car keys. She was needed on set; dawn was breaking around the edges of the towel I used as a curtain.

"If she e-mails you again," she said, "tell me right away."

"Yes," I said. I was still sitting on my mattress. I got on my knees and looked up at her. "The instant she e-mails me again, I'll tell you." I pulled down Carla's pants. I fucked Carla even though she didn't have time. We said, "I love you."

■  ■  ■

The next night, Carla showed me *The Story of Adele H*. It was about a celebrity's daughter who went mad stalking a soldier who ignored her. The movie didn't say it, but what it was about was that she got hotter and hotter the madder she became, wandering North American colonies in a green dress.

"I didn't realize how problematic this movie was when I was a kid," said Carla. "I just thought, I'm unlovable, like her. All the world will attend my dad's funeral while I'm in an asylum, like her. I'll always be obscure and alone, like her."

What I liked about the movie, I said, was that the girl had no reason to like the guy. She didn't know him.

"Of course not," said Carla. "It's easier to be obsessed with someone when you don't know them. You make them into whatever it is you want."

When Carla fell asleep, I went to the bathroom, sat on the toilet, opened the e-mail from Olive, and hit reply. *It means a lot to hear you say that*, I wrote, and hit send.

In the morning, she wrote back. "Uh-oh," I called to Carla. "Here comes Olive." Carla came to look at my phone with her toothbrush arrested in her mouth. She read the e-mail I'd sent to Olive. Then she read Olive's response:

> *I miss you, Nutella. And I'm worried about you. You haven't had an easy path. I'm here, you know, if you ever want to have a drink and talk about how things are going.*

Carla paced. She took a small bag of pretzels from her purse, tore it open, and put a pretzel in her mouth. "Fuck her," she said, eating. "You're her ex. We've all been there. What the fuck." I struggled to suppress a grin. Having succeeded in making Carla jealous, I felt as if I were seated in the cockpit of a fighter plane, a lethal machine I could halfway control.

■   ■   ■

"I have a question about frats," said Carla. My Delta Zeta Chi sweatshirt was lying on the bathroom floor, where she'd dropped it on the way into the shower. She'd put on the clothes she'd brought in her overnight bag and she was strafing the hair at the nape of her neck with the blow-dryer she kept in my dresser.

"Ask me anything you want," I said.

"You're nice," she said. "But frat boys are fucked up. Every day there's some story on the internet about something disgusting being done to some girl in a frat house, or some shitty thing they did to each other. Did you do stuff like that? Or are you the one nice one?"

I said that when the right guys are running a fraternity, it's a place where people will tell you if you're being an asshole. The instant you do something obnoxious, you get called on it. It's like having twenty older brothers who're there to help you grow up. But if the wrong guys are running a fraternity it's more like a barbarian tribe, where all that matters is whether you're in it or not. If you're in it you can do what you want and all the others will stand behind you. A kid who's insecure, who's been kicked around and left out his whole life, he suddenly has that and he gets high. He does something terrible to a girl to remind himself that he has it. Maybe that's even the appeal he has, for some girl he's trying to seduce: the way he walks and talks and wipes his ass, it's all done with a certain confidence, because he knows he's special now. It's not all his fault, necessarily. He picks it up from the atmosphere.

· · ·

*Dear Caleb,*

*Please accept my sincere apologies for the e-mails I've sent you over the past few days. I regret the intrusion and promise it will not continue.*

*Sincerely,*

*Olive*

A few hours after I received the e-mail, Carla knocked on my door. It was dusk, and she was tired from a day of meetings, her makeup imperfectly removed. A stroke of eyeliner darkened her left eye. Her MacBook was tucked under her arm. We had plans to watch the beginning of *Fanny and Alexander*, which I'd never seen, and she had it on her hard drive. I unlocked the door and sat on my mattress, waiting.

She walked past me into my apartment. She took a bottle of Sancerre from her bag. Next, two cucumber-and-egg-salad sandwiches from craft services or a restaurant, wrapped in wax paper. She placed them at my feet, on the carpet.

I didn't say anything. She shifted her weight from one foot to the other. "Let's not eat these sandwiches, actually," she said. "I don't know what I was thinking. Let's have dinner somewhere really amazing. It's my treat. I insist."

"Okay," I said.

Carla drove. The Lincoln's engine snarled as we ascended a hill beside a lake full of idle rowboats and merged with the northbound 101. The silhouetted tops of palm trees hovered like spiders in the sky.

"I didn't tell them to fire her," said Carla. "They're not going to fire her. I said it shouldn't be a punitive approach we took, just, let's figure out how we can get along, going forward."

A nearby car was playing a radio show about cooking. Then we broke free of traffic and were alone with the sound of the engine and the damp air in our faces.

"What did you do?" I asked.

Carla rolled up her window. She'd had her agent, who was Olive's boss, get Olive on a conference call, she said. "It was short. She cried. She was like, 'I'm sorry, I'm sorry.'"

"You forced her to apologize to me," I said. "You forced her to stop e-mailing me."

Carla said nothing. She looked at the road and drummed her fingers on the wheel. I told her to take the next exit, and we sank into a lowland of fast food and half-gentrified strip malls. I told her to pull into a parking lot shared by a pharmacy, a Laundromat, and a gelateria.

Once she'd parked the car, she cut the engine and put her hands in the air. "I have a problem with jealousy," she said. "I'm sorry I hurt someone, but I acknowledge it, and I will try to get better. I'm sorry." I didn't say anything. "No, really," she said. "I'll go to therapy. We can do couples therapy. I want to get better."

"Stop," I said. "It's okay."

She looked confused. "I'm being sincere. Maybe this could be an important wake-up call. If I work really hard, maybe it will bring us closer. We could get to a more honest place."

Why didn't I take her hand and say, *Yes, let's try*? At the time, I was only aware that I couldn't bring myself to look her in the eye or continue the conversation. Now I think I was ashamed of what my love was built on. I was so ashamed I could only form the most generic sentences. "This can't work," I said. "I'm sorry." I told her I would miss her, and that I would treasure the time we'd spent together.

I opened the door. Behind me, Carla started to cry. The landscape whipped and sharpened as if it were the screen of an old television that had been smacked; I wondered if I was crying. A sunburned family paraded from the pharmacy in white T-shirts, a boy bucking in the seat of a shopping cart like a knight riding a horse into a valley. The streetlamps were dimmed by fog.

"Why are you walking away from me?" asked Carla. She was calling me "sweetie," softer and softer.

■　■　■

People ask me what Carla was like, and I think, what *was* Carla like? I don't know. What she was like was: Carla is talking to me. That's Carla's body. Carla is educating me. I just made Carla laugh. Carla is taking me out for my birthday dinner; that's actually Carla sitting across from me, with the white bluffs behind her. That's actually Carla on the toilet. That's actually Carla identifying a homeless guy as our baby and crying at her joke. That's really Carla at the kitchen island, eating strawberries with the greens still on, depositing the greens and the surrounding flesh on the orange tile.

I wonder if Carla watched herself the way I watched her, the way the fan at the hot dog stand watched. Maybe she thought, *Now, I, Carla, spread mustard and relish on the hot dog. I am really Carla, picking out a cactus for the windowsill. I am really Carla, in my trailer on set, listening to country music from the forties, lying on the floor with my legs propped up on the chair, my book on my stomach. I, Carla, am reading a novel, a present from my father, who always knew I would be an artist. I, actually Carla, look up from the book to note the way that the light bulb casts a ring on the surface of the coffee when I tilt the paper cup.*

I dated her for eighteen months, and I don't know what she was like. I wasn't—I'm realizing this for the first time as I say it—I wasn't interested. I wasn't paying attention to what she was like. What she was like was not the point for me.

# OLLIE
# THE OWL

We should not have let the alumnus in the house. He was random. He said he lived out in the Berkshires, and he pulled up in this new Porsche at two miles per hour. His khakis had mustard stains on them, and he wore loafers even though there was snow on the ground. He was in Delta Zeta Chi when they played football in chain mail on horseback or something, so of course he loved our mascot, Ollie the Owl. The Ollie the Owl statue was the only thing about the house that was still the same from when he was in it.

Now he's got this routine. He goes up to the "secret attic" and puts his hand on the thing's head and says, "How's it hangin', Ollie?" like he's figured out the cool way to say hello to a wooden bird. Then he eats lunch downstairs, a tuna sandwich he brings in a Ziploc bag, and asks us about our service to the community.

"Just keeping watch over the place," he says. Then he reminds us what our motto is, even though it's on a plaque three feet from his head: CHALLENGING EACH MAN TO A GREATER WORTH SERVING ALWAYS JUSTICE AND THE GREATER GOOD.

And nobody wants to say it, but it's like, that was 150 years ago somebody made that up. Not to be negative. But I mean, we're young guys. What are we supposed to do? Is this some movie where a cool frat saves the school from a guy named Dean Mordoch or whatever? What are we supposed to serve? Nobody really ever gives a shit, actually, but he's like, "I heard one of you made a little bozo of himself during a protest march. Some kind of song and dance where you showed your down-stairs." He doesn't say any names, but Swordfish starts acting extra-casual, crossing his arms and playing with the brim of his cap. Because during the Women's Center Take Back the Night march he danced on the balcony with a black strap-on on his head, played Marvin Gaye's "Sexual Healing" on our weather-proof iPhone station, and mooned people.

"Now, horsing around is horsing around, but how do you think showing your ass to a bunch of girls would've looked to the guys who started this whole thing? They would have had a conniption."

Swordfish walks off to his room.

"You're supposed to be brothers in honor," the alumnus continues. "You are part of an organization that was created for selflessness and service, not stripteasing on a damn balcony." He shakes his hand in the air as he says it. And then Swordfish comes out of his bedroom with the black strap-on he wore on his head during the Take Back the Night march and straps it onto Ollie the Owl, who is standing behind the alumnus.

Everyone gets quiet. The alumnus turns around and looks and doesn't move for a while. Then he walks out, down the stairs. We hear the Porsche start in the driveway.

"What?" asks Swordfish, grinning, but nobody says any-thing. We just stare at the sex toy on the wooden owl. We're all mad, don't get me wrong. It's a truly shitty thing to do. But we're not going to boot Swordfish for it, and we all know it. He's too good a guy.

When Ollie disappears during the night, we just figure somebody got pissed at Swordfish and put Ollie in his bed or something.

The next afternoon, Swordfish and I are like, let's go to the Hu Ke Lau on Comedy Buffet Night, just to go to it. And we're there with our chicken lo mein and our mai tais, and this comedian guy with a microphone says, "Dating is like mowing the lawn, isn't it, ladies?" And Swordfish does the thing where he coughs "Suck m'dick" into his hand, and this old Chinese lady is like, "Quiet please," and we're like, "Sorry, sorry, but oh excuse me, could I . . ." and then superloud, ". . . *please possibly bother you for some tea.*" Because we are all about the tea at the Hu Ke Lau. And then we come back to the house and it's, hey, feeling good, we just had some good Hu Ke Lau, and now, oh my God. Because Wolf is rolling around on his side making burbling noises.

"Brendan, what happened?" I ask. It's the first time I've called Wolf by his real name since his parents visited when he was a freshman and asked me to make sure he didn't lose his orthopedic sneakers.

"I don't know what hit me," he says. "I only saw it from up close but I think it flew."

We assume he is completely fucking with us, but he's staring straight ahead with his hoodie rolled up like a carpet so you can see his belly, and there's a stain on his jeans where he shat himself. Swordfish taps me on the shoulder.

"Look," says Swordfish, and points with his chin. The rafters are covered with little cuts, like somebody chucked a lawn mower at the ceiling a few times.

We call security and everything, and they say they'll get the guy. They don't sound that confident, though. I'm not confident and I hate more than anything else feeling not confident. Swordfish and I are on the rugby team, and before a game Coach will talk about showing the other side we have more class, and we'll all put our hands in the center of a circle and say "My strength is the strength of ten because my heart is pure" three times, like we're supposed to be thinking about being the English soldiers fighting Napoleon in a historical movie. I think when we say that, we're not actually trying to have pure hearts. We're trying to get rid of the feeling of being not confident, and that's why we play the game, to get rid of that feeling. But obviously I don't say that.

The next morning, as house manager, I call a meeting. Swordfish calls up the stairs, "Borat and Dracula, you too. This shit's for real."

Borat and Dracula are two physics majors from some country I keep forgetting. We call them that because they talk like that. We rent them two rooms in the annex of the house even though they're not Delta Zeta Chi, just to help with rent. They walk down the stairs in that I'm-not-hurrying foreigner way, with their hands in their pockets and their backs straight.

"What's the problem?" asks Dracula.

"You partied hard yesterday evening," says Borat.

"Please sit down, guys," I say. "We're here to talk about the Wolfman. He may not be a fallen brother to you, but you do live in a house with us and we share some things that happen to us."

They foreigner it over to the white couch.

"The Wolf is convalescing okay," I say. "He's at the trauma unit at Cooley Dickinson. He's got some cuts and bruises, and it was a real rough day for him, but he's going to be fine. The issue is, was anybody else possibly there when it happened and is now being shy for some reason? Because the time has now come for you to speak up."

Borat raises his hand. He takes off his glasses and scratches at something on one of the lenses. "I heard wings," he says, "and the howl of a dog through the neck of a bird."

Dracula makes the "perfect" sign and points to Borat. "Hey, this guy is precise," he says. "Howl of dog through neck of bird."

"And you just sat there upstairs, like, who cares," says Swordfish.

"Yes." Dracula shrugs. "Why leave my studies, when I think that it might only be you and your girlfriend of one weekend on a sled to hell?"

"Listen, fellas," Swordfish says to Borat and Dracula. "Just communicate as best you can what your ears were trying to tell you. The rest of us are here to listen." Swordfish wants to do international law, not finance like me and Wolf and Laser. He has a diplomacy complex. He leans forward and puts his hands together.

I lean forward and put my hands together as well, so that we are all almost touching foreheads. "This is probably not the way it is in every culture," I say. "But here, if somebody is hurt, and other people might get hurt, that's considered significant, and you have to tell the truth."

Borat sighs and makes a brushing-aside motion with his hand. "You have a monster," he says. "You did something to make him come."

Swordfish and I are sitting in this talk-show healing way, so we can't laugh, but everybody else does—Laser, Nighttrain, Buckhunter, and Ironman. Borat and Dracula sit back on the white couch and cross their arms across their chests.

"Let's think of that as the worst-case scenario but not necessarily likely," I say.

"Okay," says Swordfish. "Next order of business, then. How many people here think it was some crazy fucker like Christina Richman?"

Christina Richman is this student-newspaper girl who's always writing editorials saying frats should be shut down. She devoted considerable space to Swordfish's behavior during the Take Back the Night march, and he's been fixated on her ever since. For my part, I simply think she's not living up to her potential as far as hotness is concerned.

"She is neither crazy nor fucker," says Borat, straightening his back. We all get quiet for a moment, registering that Borat likes Christina Richman.

"Stop with the Christina Richman already," says Ironman finally.

"Fuck her, man," says Swordfish, staring into space. "She's like, 'Frats are discriminatory,' but if she would just get contact lenses and put on a little makeup, then she'd be hot, and we'd let her into our parties."

Borat whispers something to himself in his grunty language.

"Does anybody else have any other ideas?" I ask. Nobody does, and I'm still not confident.

So Swordfish and I go cross-country skiing. We started to do that together when we ran into each other once on the Robert Frost Trail, both using sets our moms gave us. We just follow the trails for a couple hours and then go home and usually have some cocoa with marshmallows and play foosball.

We're out by this brook and we ski past a flock of brown birds. It's more like we ski through them; they're coming right toward us, or just blowing around us, the most motivated flock of birds I've ever seen. They're making this little high, panicked sound, and then they're past us already. Then, from way off, we hear the wings of something bigger.

We've both stopped skiing. The sound is a little closer now, near the old yellow brick smokestacks that pop up over the trees on the edge of the trail.

"You know what's funny?" asks Swordfish. "I'm kind of obsessing over what Borat and Dracula said."

And then I hear it: the howl of a dog through the neck of a bird. I turn around and see the thing for the first time.

It comes down on Swordfish. I realize I've thrown myself to the ground and I'm lying on my side. I start to unbuckle my skis. Swordfish is making this sound like he's puking, and the thing on top of him is concentrating and quiet.

It's wooden, and dwarf-size. It has claws at the bottom and a face that's a perfect circle, only all made out of wooden feathers, with big wooden circle eyes. The lids are like upside-down teacups, and they click up and down. The eyes beneath them are splintery holes. Its wings are short, and when it hunches—it's hunched over Swordfish—its head pumps in and out of its neck. It's weird to watch wood move like an animal, the way an animal kind of pulses around.

I stand up in my ski boots and grab the ski behind me. I swing it way back and bring it down on the thing's head. The owl—because now I can see that's what it is—makes its dog-bird sound. I tackle it, and it shakes like a laundry machine does when it has a broken belt.

Then I feel something where I shouldn't feel anything, moving up and down. Swordfish is pale. There's puke on his face. "Look," he says. He points at what's moving, and I recognize it immediately. I pull away and stumble backward through the snow, staring at Ollie the Owl, who has come alive because of the strap-on.

It makes the noise at me again and curls over Swordfish. I realize what it's doing, now that I know what I'm looking at.

"Swordfish," I say. "Take your skis off, so you can stand up. Let it try to do what it wants to do to you, just for a second."

Swordfish fumbles with his skis and it humps at him the way a dog humps at your leg. I grab a rock and bang it off its head. Then Swordfish gets to his feet and I go at it with my ski again, only this time I hit it down there. It makes the sound, beats its wings, and glides away over the trees toward the yellow smokestacks. We run.

———

"Slyepoi Mongol, the Blind Mongol," says Dracula. "That is with what you have fallen sick."

Because they've known since the meeting our house has a demon, they've moved temporarily into Cross-Cultural House. We're sitting in the really clean kitchen drinking tea. Borat pokes his head upstairs to make sure nobody else is home.

"Isn't that word kind of racist?" asks Swordfish.

"Slyepsi Uregh," says Borat. He picks up a plastic-covered dictionary and flips through it until he finds something. "This means, in English, the Blind Thruster, the Blind Piercer. From the Old Church Slavonic language. In later Slav stories, it becomes a Mongol. A very old demon, but in a later time they do not call a demon a demon."

Dracula nods and puts a sugar cube between his teeth. He sips his tea and the cube turns red.

"The demon has a sex never vanquished," Borat continues. "Because it is blind, it thrusts but its member never finds a home." He unwraps a Snickers he was carrying in his pocket and dunks it.

Swordfish puts his head in his hands. "How do you know it's not just some weird bird?" he asks. He rubs his eyes. "How about this. You come out to the woods with us and tell us whether you still think it's the blind thing. I'll make it worth your while."

"There is nothing worth it," says Borat.

"All it actually does is try to fuck you," says Swordfish. He leans in. "Look, these names that we use for you and Dracula can sometimes sound negative, or like we're making fun of you, but we use them on you because you're our really good friends. You live under the same roof with us, and we think of you as honorary brothers. Just go on a walk in the woods with us and tell us what's going on."

Borat's eyebrows shoot up. "You have Christina Richman come to the house while I'm in the kitchen, you have a bargain."

Swordfish's mouth falls open a little bit. He takes off his cap and rubs it.

"You have a crush on her?" I ask Borat.

Dracula nods.


We tell Christina Richman we'll give her an exclusive on our attitudes about gender. She comes over, and I'm like, "Let's maybe talk in the kitchen, so you can see we're exploring our feminine sides," which is a good one, and Borat's waiting there, as we walk in. Soon, she and Borat are standing next to each other by the cutting board looking through some Afghanistan photo book someone had to check out from the library for class. They're pointing at things in it, and Christina is saying something about the infant mortality rates with her hands pushed way down in the pockets of her overalls, and Borat has his arms folded really tightly across this zip-up sweater he went out and bought. Dracula goes into his room and comes back with more photo books, which he puts on the table and backs away from.

Then there's a high fluty sound, outside, maybe down by the soccer fields. The next moment the owl bangs against the window, like birds do. Christina makes a hyperventilating noise. Borat says something to himself in his language that you can tell is probably a swear. It bangs against the side of the house, and plates fall down and break on the Afghanistan book. I run to the front door and lock it, knocking over a chair on the way, which knocks over a lamp, which knocks our mounted Frank Sinatra mug-shot poster off the wall. I put my shoulder to the door just in time, because the owl bangs into the door hard enough that my shoulder feels like it's going to crack. There are tears in my eyes and I want to run away.

I look back inside the room to see who could take my place. Borat's like seven feet tall but built like a centipede. Dracula's more of a soft pod. Christina is chewing on a strand of her hair. I turn to Swordfish. Compared to the others, he and I are built like a different species. We're rugby players. I mean, it hurts us to get hit, but when you look at our bodies you can tell we were meant to do this. This is like childbirth for us, our painful but natural role in the universe.

"Swordfish," I say, and he stumbles over. We both know what we're going to do. There's not really a choice.

"Fuck you, blindman assfucker," I shout, and when I shout it I can feel how old the words are, from the way they scratch the bottom of my throat. I open the door and Swordfish runs outside. I follow him, and it claws at our chests. As it scratches me, I try to screw off its head.

But Swordfish has a different idea. He has both hands on the strap-on, and he's reaching around to the back. I see his hand fumble with the clasp. I try to help him with it but the owl screams in my ear so loud I lose my grip and fall back. I look down at my body and there's blood dripping down my shirt.

Then I look up and see Swordfish. He's holding the strap-on, still attached to Ollie, who has lifted off. For a bit the wings go extra-fast, to achieve the proper altitude, and then it soars, Swordfish dangling and still reaching for the clasps. They go up over the house, toward the red sky, through these black dead trees, and when Swordfish's legs hit a branch, the snow shakes off.

Over the soccer field, Swordfish falls, silhouetted by the setting winter sun. I run down the man-made hill to where he lies. He's on his back, holding the strap-on. I kneel beside him.

"Christina Richman," he says. "Tell her."

"Tell her what?" I take his hand.

"That I sweat her. Sweated." His eyes close. He releases my hand and holds the strap-on tight against himself.

After the ambulance comes we find Ollie the Owl, with its wings folded, about fifty feet away, by the tennis courts. I never realized it before, but it always looks like it's sleeping. Borat, Dracula, and I bury it by the generator near the Robert Frost Trail.

Swordfish's parents freak out at his funeral. His bald dad puts his hands on the sides of his head, by the tufts of hair around his ears, looking down into the casket, in this room with really thick brown fleur-de-lis wallpaper, and says, Oh my God, Oh my God, and keeps looking down there. Swordfish's mom and aunt walk him out of the room and lower him onto a bench in the hall, where he sits the way Swordfish used to sit sometimes, with his legs spread and his head in his hands.

Borat is in the next room, holding hands with Christina Richman. I want to say what I'm supposed to say to Christina Richman but obviously I don't. When Swordfish's mom and aunt go to talk to Coach, who gives them this photo of

Swordfish smiling with his mouth guard in, I sit next to Swordfish's dad on the bench and try to think of something to say.

I'm thinking this, as I look at Swordfish's dad: Now, when I look up and focus on nothing in particular and the geese are over the library tower, I can hear things. Like the feral cats that gnaw the pizza boxes that we lean against the house on recycling day are asking for help. Even like, when I look at something like the shitty houses with the brown lawns by Route 9, all the powerless things are asking for me, like there are these tiny fingers everywhere reaching out. But obviously I don't say that.

# THE
# TREASURER

When one of Pete's fraternity brothers posted the video to a closed Greek Facebook group, people said that what happened in the video was rape. At first Pete thought the commenters meant that he had raped the girl. But then he scrolled down and realized they considered him the victim.

It hadn't occurred to him to think of himself as having been raped any more than it had occurred to him to think of himself as a rapist. He rose from his swivel chair and looked in the mirror. His polo shirt still hugged his gut tighter than it hugged his pecs. His curls were still dark and springy. He still had abundant ear hair, and chubby cheeks. He took off his clothes, held his shoulders, ass, thighs, and package. In this way he confirmed that he was still Petey, whom everybody loved.

By the time the event captured in the video took place, he was used to being the object of disrespectful acts. In Delta, having disrespectful things done to you was a pathway to prestige. When you were a pledge, you did the whale, where the actives bailed pissed-in water from the toilet, poured it in the sink, and made you blow bubbles in it. When you surfaced, you recited the names of ten actives. If you did it without complaint, you got to become an active yourself.

It was a similar deal when he had a girlfriend sophomore

year. Once word got out, they made him sit in the crab apple tree wearing an apricot taffeta gown they kept in the basement. After a few hours they let him come down, and everyone shook his hand. No one ever really gave him any shit after that. Everyone in Delta who had a steady girlfriend had had to do the same thing; it was a way to prove that even though you had a girlfriend you still had self-esteem, because an insecure douche would have refused to put on a dress. An insecure douche would have refused to get in the tree.

When Pete was elected treasurer at the beginning of his senior year, having crushed a junior who'd spoken of "planting seeds" and making Delta a "lean start-up, not a government," he knew that he would have to pass another test of character before his inauguration. Every Delta voted into leadership had to weather a ceremony designed to test his confidence. For some it was a gauntlet of slaps, for others butt-chugging, in which vodka was funneled through a broken bottle into the anus, for others eight hours on all fours.

The party where it happened was like all other members-only Delta parties: Kendrick and a keg hose coiled in its nest, ska and the aftertaste of Domino's garlic bread. Pete no longer found such parties exciting, but they were comforting, evenings spent among friends. They were the kind of fun he had yearned for back in high school, when he'd forced himself to spend his evenings alone, hoping to grind his way into an Ivy, trying in vain to bring up his grades. He passed hundreds of hours staring at the homework modules, unable to complete them; they all required web-based research, and when he was online he couldn't not go on Facebook and Instagram to see what people were up to—making space for grief after the death of a dog, or posting photos of a caf worker whose mis-labeled milks had compromised a vegan—so that by the time he thought to return to the window where the module lay in wait for him, he had to remind himself what he was supposed to be learning about, and after he had reoriented his attention so much time had passed that he had to check his feeds again. Adderall was helpful and then less so. He learned the hard way that he couldn't focus on anything if there was no one around to watch him focus. His one victory was to lose ten pounds and keep them off, using a step machine his mother had aban-doned. As he climbed, he listened to Spotify and imagined that every band was an attic quartet consisting of himself and his future friends at Dartmouth: a troubled friend on vocals, a practical friend on drums, a studious black friend with wire-rimmed glasses on guitar, and he, Petey, on bass. A bassist, he felt, was a motor, a shortstop, and a mother.

The party had been going strong for three hours when the headlights of a 4Runner lit the street in front of the house. A short woman hopped from the driver's seat. She was broad-shouldered, with hair that hung straight like Snoopy's ears, and she was older than Pete, twenty-six or thirty; he could never read grown-ups' ages. It was warm, early October, but she wore a trench coat with a floppy belt. She walked briskly with her hands in the coat's pockets, chin up, pug nose horizontally creased. She had that pleasing aspect that female rugby players had, especially the short ones, of seeming dense in the flesh. She looked like she could thrust from a ruck with her eyes on the grass and pound the crown of her head into an interloper's face. There was a long, heavy-looking gray bag thrown over her shoulder, and she wouldn't let anyone help her with it as she walked up the soft, creaking steps and slipped through the smokers on the porch.

When she reached the living room she conferred with Gavin, the vice president of social programming, businesslike with her hands on her hips. He pointed and she dropped the bag with a swish of nylon and a bell-like clang.

On her knees she removed three telescoping cylinders, which, when joined via spring-loaded knobs, composed a pole, to which she locked a square plate at either end with a hex key. She stood on a chair to tap the ceiling for a joist and made the top plate exert upward pressure by cranking a screw with a wrench that had been stored in a wrench-shaped pocket in the bag's interior. In essence, the stripper pole was a curtain rod, friction fit between ceiling and floor. She shook it with both hands. Judging it steady, she vanished into the bathroom. Gavin lowered the shades. He summoned all present and put on Marilyn Manson, and as if conjured by the music, the girl minced out bare-breasted in a silver skirt. The crease in her nose remained as she gripped the pole with four limbs and revolved. It was, Pete felt, the crease in her nose that his brothers cheered, or the mix of smooth performance and frank disgust.

When the dance was over, Gavin took Pete by the elbow and escorted him to the bathroom from which the dancer had emerged. Once a scrawny, slope-shouldered boy, Gavin had widened and hardened at the age of twenty. He had shorn off his hair, and the result was warlike majesty. Shortly after he'd become attractive, Gavin had become quiet. You could barely hear him. "Go ahead and take your pants and shirt off, Petey," he said, standing in the doorframe. When he smiled, the bathroom brightened, and his voice grew even softer. "I'd rather not do it for you, even though you're a beautiful man." That was when Pete knew for certain that the ritual performed on him that night would be more frightening than the whale, and that the dancer would be part of it.

Sitting on the furred toilet seat, untying his shoes, Pete could hear, through the wall, the hiss of a mattress being manhandled down the stairs. The line of light beneath the door went dim. The music died. The crowd sound came through clearly now, a congenial drone pricked by squeals. Even in the bathroom, there were faint notes of beer, weed, cider, and cologne, good smells that spoiled when they were steeped in one another. Someone shouted, "And I was like, 'Until you know the Dead, don't judge the Dead.'"

Gavin opened the door for Pete and extended his arm toward the living room in a gesture of welcome. On the mattress, surrounded by his fellow seniors save for a path that cleared before him, the girl lay naked on her back. A floor lamp had been placed near her legs; he could see the calluses on the soles of her heels. Her lavender-nailed fingers drummed on the white sheet.

Gavin raised his hand for silence. He took out his phone and read from it.

"Hear ye, hear ye," he said at the volume of normal conversation. "This is Jane, a dancer from Electric Blue." There was applause.

"Petey"—Gavin turned to Pete—"you are treasurer-elect of this great chapter of Delta Zeta Chi. I command you to go forth and prove your faithfulness by giving your finest cunnilingus to this girl." The dancer seemed to sneeze, as she brought her hand briefly to her face, but Pete couldn't hear anything for the thunderous clapping, so it was hard to be sure.

He stood for a moment with his arms folded across his chest and approached the dancer slowly, because he felt that it was possible she would be so repulsed by his body that she would decide she couldn't go through with the gig. It was important to give her ample avenue for retreat.

He knelt between her legs, which were bruised on the shins and pink around the knees. While he'd been worried that she would sneer at him, or roll her eyes, he could see her face now, and the set of her mouth was neutral and she blinked rapidly as if tempted to sleep. He supposed that she was spacing out, thinking of something other than what she was doing and where she was.

When he went down on her, she was still and unresponsive, which made him feel inept and ugly. Her labia tasted like crying and fingertips. They brandished fewer affectations than his ex-girlfriend's labia, which had smelled powdered, somehow, and had had less hair. His erection was as hard and relentless as the erections he'd had in late puberty: the seventh-grade erections on the morning bus, the erections thudding at the underside of *Harry Potter and the Deathly Hallows*, the erections that had refused to slacken during his oral presentations on Vietnam and the guillotine. Those erections had filled him with the sense of a newborn power even as they filled him with fear. But this was different. For if he got an erection from doing something he was forced to do, it must mean that he longed to be forced to do things.

In order to avoid thinking about this, he pursued the same tack the girl seemed to have chosen: he urged his mind to wander. He tunneled back through the years to winters in overheated hallways, stains on perforated ceilings, that is, to high school. Not to his high school per se but to the Young Judaea Northeast Weekend Convention of 2012, for which Young Judaea had rented a school building from a district in inner Hartford, a fortress replete with basketball courts and media rooms. There, he and Dorit Gilad had become friends. They skipped nearly all of the classes, in which you were occasionally asked to share what Israel meant to you, and roamed an adultless landscape, or rather a landscape where the adults in charge were watchful but invisible, which seemed very Israel. They complained about the students at their schools who circulated boycott petitions—this was pro forma commiseration at YJ, nothing more than small talk—until it was night outside the barred windows. That was when they stumbled on a secluded teachers' lounge with an old DVD player wired to an ancient television perched on a portable rack. The disc tray contained episode 1 of a PBS documentary, *The Civil War*, which they watched not seated in any of the various desk chairs but sprawled with their backs to the carpet, looking up. Bearded, apprehensive generals shone down like moons. Twenty minutes in, he felt he could touch her, and, intending to reach around her head and hold her shoulder—he thought of a Union soldier in a photograph, resting his hand on the shoulder of his wife—he rested his hand on her breast by mistake. It took him a minute to realize what had happened, because he had never held a breast before, and when he saw where his hand was he withdrew it, which was insane because she had already allowed it to be there. She neither moved nor spoke. They lay in the dark and watched the nation sink into bloodshed.

Why was it, he wondered, as the cheers of "Petey" grew and flagged, grew and flagged, that he thought of Dorit now, six years later? He could still feel the heat of her breast in his hand. Perhaps it was because tonight was like that night in Hartford, in that an organization had facilitated his hooking up with a girl he might not otherwise have hooked up with. A stated aim of Young Judaea, after all, had been to help Jewish teens befriend other Jewish teens. So that, when he reached for Dorit, it wasn't just a private charge running between two people but, like the present exercise, a submission to tribal will. And it was always that sense of his body being part of a larger body, of his being locked within a host and doing its bidding, that had been the warmest feeling of his life.

The dancer, perhaps in response to a cue from Gavin, pressed down on Pete's head with both hands. It was difficult for Pete to breathe. The cheering intensified. She released his head and depressed it repeatedly, giving him chances to recover between applications of force, and the fourth or fifth time she held him down, she made things simpler—she tipped his face so that his mouth rested above her genitals. Now he could do nothing but bury his nose in her stomach. We're in this together, she seemed to say, so let's make it easier on both of us. He closed his eyes. She released and pressed him again, and the noise of the crowd rose and lapsed with her efforts. He guessed that this was a big finish that Gavin had arranged. She was making faces, he gathered, pretending to have an orgasm. It wouldn't make for a good ending if she just said, *Okay, we're done now.* After another thirty seconds of climax, she freed him, and Gavin helped him to his feet, holding up his hand as though he had boxed and won.

His brothers gathered round to congratulate him. He looked past them at the dancer. She was putting on her clothes, sitting on the stairs, her jeans already on. Gavin gave her a wad of bills. She counted the money and tucked it into the front pocket of the bag in which she carried the pole.

The pole must have been disassembled, for he could see its tubes straining the bag's fabric. Wait, thought Pete, don't go. But he said nothing. It was unclear to him what there was to say.

Gavin drew him aside. "I want you to know," he said, "that when we went to make the deal, we asked her if she was clean in the region, and she said, no question, she'd been tested. That's the reason we drove all the way to Electric Blue to find a girl, instead of just going to Castaway, because our conversations were always about safety."

"How much did you pay her?" Pete asked.

"Six hundred."

In the morning he sat with the outgoing treasurer, Tom McCreary, to learn the job. Tom sat at the breakfast table eating waffles with his hands, dipping chunks in a puddle of syrup that covered his plate. He talked Pete through the Excel spreadsheet you used for reconciling the Delta Mastercard on the fifteenth of every month and showed him how to process purchase orders through the national headquarters in Maryland. Cool sunlight blanched the Ikea table, and crisp leaves blew into the kitchen whenever someone opened the door to the backyard. Despite last night's moments of wretchedness, he felt a stirring of loyalty. Here was Tom, twenty-one like him, and yet already managing the money for a house of thirty students, when most people their age were still children, living only for themselves. Soon it would be Pete who carried the Mastercard in his wallet. Soon it would be Pete cracking down on actives who tapped the petty cash for food and gave their meal-plan points to girls. If he chose, he could never think about the dancer again. He could laugh if someone brought her up.

It was after he'd showered and shaved, sitting in his attic room freshly dressed, that he read the comments on the closed Greek Facebook group. First there were girls posting, *rape, this is absolutely rape, yes, rape,* and so on. But then there was an argument, with the participants divided according to gender.

The girls said:

*I love love love guys, especially Deltas, but I will never understand them. Pay a stripper to assault one of your actives? Great idea. Just explain to me, why?*

*Guaranteed fucking genius way to catch mouth herpes.*

*There is nothing voluntary about this, as far as I can tell. She's holding him down and potentially giving him diseases.*

*Is it still rape if he consented to that, but from peer pressure? That's when it becomes the campus debate of free will vs. we're all social beings.*

*Think about if it was the other way around with a girl and a guy. No one would ever think that was fine. This is not paddling or something, Deltas. Perfect strategy to make sure you never get laid, btw, just in case you're interested.*

*I love Deltas but this is beyond gay-zing into something more fucked.*

*Not hazing bc he's an active. But personally my heart goes out to this guy, his brothers should have taught him to be a man, not submit to degradation.*

The guys said:

*Cant see his face but dued looks like hes having a good time.*

*I say bring it on this guy gets to practice on a professional and and no doubt he would pay to be abel to do this*

*Truth personally myself Im jealous you might be getting herpse in the mouth virtually any time you go down on a beocth*

*The problem is the idiot who posted this theres nothing inaprropriate about this but keep it IN THE HOSUE. Whats the point of having one? Its so you can do fun shit and maintain your discretion.*

Some of the guys, he suspected, wrote their comments normally and then added typos and misspellings. That was what he usually did.

After he'd inspected his body and held portions of it in both hands and reassured himself that he was still himself, he decided to stop sulking and put on his clothes. The thing was, if all you saw was the video, what you saw was the dancer pressing his head into her crotch and pretending to come. You didn't see the dancer wrinkle her nose in her reluctance to climb the front steps. Was it not possible for two people to sort of rape each other at the same time, with success? What had happened between him and the dancer was a transaction. She was a businessperson and he was a future businessperson.

He went to Electric Blue's website to see if it had any information on Jane. There was in fact a page titled "Dancer Profiles," though there were only two dancers listed.

PORTIA:

The daughter of three generations of eminent businesspeople from the Old Saybrook area. She represents both the eros and ambition of the cafe.

ERIN:

A practitioner of arts and crafts, Erin operates her own web company. She enjoys pressing flowers and genealogy.

A knock at the door. Gavin, in his white pajama bottoms and his white T-shirt with green sleeves and shamrocks that said HAPPY EUROPEAN N-WORD DAY. It was a shirt Gavin tended to wear, Pete knew, when he felt scared or vulnerable. He'd worn it after his autistic brother had visited the house and played foosball against himself for two hours, and then he'd worn it on and off the week before elections. He held his laptop open in front of him and kept his eyes on the screen even as he cracked the door and walked sideways into Pete's room.

"This shit on Facebook," he said. "I mean—" He closed the door behind him, shut the laptop, and put a hand on Pete's shoulder. "Tell me honestly, man. Do you feel like you got raped?"

To Pete's surprise, he hesitated. He considered the warmth of Gavin's hand on his T-shirt. For a second, he thought about trying to tell Gavin what it had been like.

"No," Pete said.

"Right?" said Gavin. "You know you liked it, dude, don't lie. When I was pitching it to the committee, I was like, 'You know Petey will love it.'" He sat on Pete's bed. "People need to respect your perspective. You see what they're saying about you?"

Pete grunted.

"The thing about it is, who cares? But if some girl who's pissed about some mildly ill shit that might have happened here a while ago sees that there's a video that's supposed to be evidence that we're the kind of guys who . . ." Because Gavin's voice was quiet, he could make it trail off gently. "You see what I'm saying? I'm getting kind of paranoid."

"Don't be," Pete said. For some reason, he laughed.

"Thank you," said Gavin. "Thank you for saying that. What I was thinking is, let me take you out to Electric Blue. What I did, according to some people, crossed the line, so I want to make it up to you. I would like to do that. Also, I was thinking, if you don't mind, while we're there, I could take a picture of you looking normal, so that I can post something on the group that's like, 'Hey you all, this is the guy you're saying got raped by that stripper, but does he look like that's how he experienced it? Does he want to be anonymous or something, like, what the actual fuck?' But mostly to say thank you."

"You don't have to take me to Electric Blue," said Pete. "I'm actually good."

"You're getting a lap dance on Delta," said Gavin. "End of conversation. If you need to move some funds from the social programming line, you can do that. You have an okay from me."

To give a foretaste of the lap dance, Gavin plucked Pete's headphones from the floor, plugged them into his own laptop, set one bud in Pete's ear, retained the other bud for himself, and played a track about bottle service, tan lines, and making it rain. They stood cheek by jowl, listening. It was, Pete had to admit, a good song. His head bobbed diagonally, in sync with Gavin's.

Electric Blue Cafe stood at the crossroads of Route 195 and I-84. Pete had passed its billboard twice, driving south on 195 to watch the Minutemen play UConn. The first time, it had been a painting of a woman with blue skin in a black bikini, reclining on a stage with her head thrown back and her hair, midnight blue, pooled on a sky-blue floor. The second time, the full-body portrait had given way to a close-up of the blue-skinned woman's face in the throes of pain or ecstasy. There was an electronic device embedded in her scalp, partially obscured by her hair; it was possible she was a sex machine. Now, the blue-skinned woman was gone altogether. In her place, three black silhouettes cavorted before a wallpaper of flames: one stalked feline on her hands and knees; a second scaled a pole like a monkey in a tree; a third squatted frog-like with her hands on the floor, her fingers spread.

Gavin took the picture when they got out of the car. It was of two boys in sunglasses in the parking lot, the club behind them, and behind the club, the setting sun. Electric Blue looked like a bunker: single-story, stucco, with blacked-out windows. In the lower branches of the trees that framed the awning there were constellations of blue Christmas lights, dim in the early evening. The facial expressions of the boys were essentially identical. Their arms were thrown around each other's shoulders, their lips were curled, their sunglasses had slipped down their noses. Their necks canted so that their foreheads touched. The members of the closed group gave the photo likes, including two of the girls who had posted that what had happened in the video was rape. It was hard not to like the photo, what with the contact between the two foreheads, the boys' open display of mutual affection, enabled by the presence of the strip club.

They showed IDs at the door and, crossing the threshold of the room, Pete had the sensation of using his face to break a cobweb. The walls were black. Blue was reserved for accents. The blue bow tie of the waitress who stood with a vibrating knife beside the carving station. The blue currency, Electric Bills. The blue backs of barstools, the blue glow of the liquor shelves, the blue light that fell from the ceiling onto silver poles, the shreds of blue ribbon glued to toothpicks. The bars that winged from either side of the stage reflected whatever color was on the flat-screens, now the whiteness surrounding the Dunkin' Donuts logo, now the tropical flash of Patriots FieldTurf. He didn't know how you could receive all the goods on offer at once—the meat, the music, the drinks, the dancers, and the sports—without them cross-contaminating, like party smells, like foods heaped from the buffet onto a single plate.

He ordered a beer and made everything fade but the contents of the spotlight.

The spotlight was the shape of an eye. It lit the dancer's skin. She was not Jane, but a fatter, darker, round-faced girl, a girl whose navel was a slit in a shivering belly. A creature more like Pete. Crouched all but naked with your body glowing, in a room full of people who wanted to look at you—that was what she did for work. That was her so-called job. He would do it for free.

# CASSIOPEIA

The grass on the Common was long and soft. You could lie down in it and sleep, and people did, with their dogs curled up beside them. If hippies had dozed off in public like that in my suburb on Long Island, the police would have shooed them away, but here you could do whatever you wanted, look however you wanted, stagger around stoned and homeless. I liked that about the town, initially. I was thrilled by the local girls my age, walking down the street on an August afternoon, their backpacks massive, their hair and nails dirty, their legs and armpits unshaved. In my high school there had been a small clique of girls whose clothes and grooming were androgynous, but people screamed at them, teachers belittled them, and the other girls were allowed to throw things at them, as long as they didn't do it very often. Here, it was normal to look like that. Everything was considered normal, here.

Sometimes, in the sweltering afternoon, a troupe of bearded men gathered on the Common in tartan skirts and danced to live accompaniment: drums, fiddle, and a flute. They were in their fifties and sixties, and there were easily twenty of them, maybe more. As a crowd gathered to watch, they greeted each other with kisses, hitched up their skirts, and kicked and pranced. In my hometown the elders professed a love of freedom but enforced a simple set of rules regarding how to spend your time, how to maintain your house and yard, how to talk, how to carry yourself, whom to sleep with, and under what circumstances. They would have grumbled at these Celtic gays, and anyway would not have preserved a village green on which a dance performance could be staged. Here you could do whatever you wanted and the townsfolk smiled. Rebellion was impossible.

The result was something that I came to call the illness, in the privacy of my thoughts. Young men and women, bare-armed, tan, circulated slowly through the streets. It wasn't only that they were idle. It was that they couldn't stop performing. A girl walked a mountain bike down the sidewalk, improvising a song about a mountain trail. Sitting on a bench in front of CVS, a boy in tie-dye beatboxed. A girl sat with her back against the Unitarian church, painting with Chinese brushes on her arm. A few feet away, a boy as young as I was, his button-down slick with sweat, tried to make passersby take an anarchist pamphlet from his hand, calling out, "Free newspaper." Whenever someone took him up on it, he asked for a donation of five dollars, in exchange for six pages, smudged, stapled, and illustrated with stick-figure cartoons. I imagined that, wherever these kids had grown up, they'd found their friends by refusing to conform. They'd belonged to tight little bands of persecuted weirdos. And even if they hadn't belonged to tight little bands, at least they'd had their persecution, which was a form of attention. Now that they found themselves in a place where nearly all behavior was acceptable, they were lonelier than they'd ever been at home.

I could feel the illness come over me. It didn't hit me right away, but by the third day of first-year orientation I could hear a change in the way I talked. In my high school I'd been regarded as unusual because I preferred *Raging Bull* to *Rocky*, progressive Democrats to moderate Republicans, Willie Nelson to Dave Matthews. I had friends who felt the same way, three boys and a girl, and the other kids called us the snobs. We walked the hallways five abreast, nursing a sense of superiority even as we kept our shoulders hunched and our faces downcast and submissive. Here, a snob was as common as a dandelion, and I began to present myself to the other kids in my dorm as a guy from Long Island; I emphasized the *g* in *Long*, and called myself a guido, neither of which I had ever done before. I wasn't even fully Italian. Most of my mother's family was Irish and Czech. But it was a handle to hold: Italian American Long Islander.

In the evenings I drove out into the farmland, past the tobacco fields on the flats near the river. The soil up here was so rich it could grow crops that grew in the South. Back in Suffolk County, I realized, the grass and trees had the spiky look of things that grew by the sea. The ocean breezes scoured the land and kept it clean. Now I was in a valley. The woods were thick as jungle, the air was half steam. Holsteins stood dazed on the hills that dribbled down to the corn. Everything was calm and cloudy, like the voices of the hippies and the water in the ponds. I stayed in my car, driving fast but in no hurry to get anywhere, singing along to the radio with the AC blowing in my face, a can of Red Bull sweating in my hand.

On my third night in town, I found a dialogue written in chalk. It was at the corner where two fraternity houses, Pike and Delta, lorded over a motel, a Korean church, and the new economics building. The exchange began at the foot of Pike's wooden Greek Revival porch, in red block letters with purple borders:

RUSH WEEK
ARE YOU IN?
HELL YES WHEN IS IT
NEXT WEEK CHIEF

The rebuttal was forest green. It started where Delta's front yard met the sidewalk. The letters were tall, straight, and plain, all virtuous simplicity.

SHUT DOWN
THE FRATS
THE SYSTEM
MUST DIE

I'd never given frats much thought. But it was nice to see that there were people who lived here who were hated by some other people who lived here.

I mentioned this to a girl in my orientation group named Adrienne. As our group leader drove us from the swimming hole to the Emily Dickinson house to the bakery, we slumped in the back of the van and exchanged complaints about the things we saw, our feet pressed against the seats in front of us, picking at the name tag stickers on our chests. We'd been struggling to find things to say: How could people eat burritos

with yogurt in them? How could there be enough terrible people, in this small town, to sustain a typewriter store? She had
thick dark eyebrows, olive skin, and shoulder-length hair that
was straight and heavy, as if its natural oils had been allowed
to accumulate. It made me think of the word *languish*. It was
languishing.

"The thing about it is," I said, "everything here is so, 'I'm
cool with you, you're cool with me,' and it's good to have a
break from it. I don't want to join a frat, but when everybody's
tolerant of everybody else it's like—" I struggled to explain.
"They're talking past each other."

Her eyes widened with pleasure. In bringing up fraternities
I'd brought up something to rant about, and a rant promised
to cut through the awkwardness of our conversation. "Fuck
those people," she said, twirling a blade of grass between her
thumb and forefinger. "The thing about them that annoys me
most isn't even necessarily the hating women, because that's
everywhere, it's that they've built these little worlds for themselves where they're kings of shit." She was suddenly beautiful
and seemed to address the passing scenery outside the window,
rather than me. "They're like nerds playing Dungeons & Drag-
ons, calling themselves knights and wizards, but they think
they're these major players. 'Did you know I'm the grand president of Phi Alpha Epsilon?' 'Did you know I'm the hottest guy
in the world, because everyone in this house agrees I'm vice
chancellor of Gamma Zeta?' It's the same with sorority girls.
'I'm not just some girl from Wayland, I'm Queen Cassiopeia
of Kappa Delta, and everyone else in this little house I live in
agrees I'm the most significant person of all time.' It's like, have

fun in your little playpen where you're all noble rulers of your little turd mountain." She thrust her hand through the van's half-open window, released the blade of grass, and flexed her fingers.

The van stopped in front of Barts Ice Cream. Everyone in the group went inside and lined up beside an old-fashioned gumball machine and a nearly life-size statue of a cow. "Barts," said Adrienne. She sneered. "Here in Amherst, they think Barts is what it's all about." She listed the ice cream parlors of her native Boston, counting them off, as if the slow recitation of their names—J.P. Licks, Toscanini's, Christina's, Emack & Bolio's— could convey the superiority of their product. She shook her head in a pantomime of melancholy. That was the real thing, she said. Barts was the one choice they had here, so they had to love it. Did we have good ice cream on Long Island?

I racked my brain. Surely I could come up with a family-owned ice cream parlor when I really needed one. There must have been some white clapboard shack with a line of parents and children waiting their turn with sandy feet, snaking down toward the Sound or the open sea. There must have been some marble-countered soda fountain with an operatic Italian name or a vaudevillian Jewish one. The problem was that I had only decided a few days ago that Long Island was important to me. I hadn't cared all that much about Long Island while I was living on it, so I hadn't paid close attention to what it was like.

Adrienne stood there looking up at me, neither my superior nor my inferior in magnetism and looks. We emitted the same amount of charge. We were both beaverish white people with prominent teeth and pouch faces, both of us on the short side, with wide hips. Perhaps this accounted for our loneliness, and therefore our susceptibility to the illness, her shoddy Bostonianism and my shoddy Long Islanderism. We weren't ugly. It was just that God hadn't set us down on Earth to be main characters. Think of a romantic comedy—there's often a secondary couple, a funnier, less important one, sometimes lustier and more cheerful than the primary couple but always less graceful, less aristocratic in bearing. We each knew ourselves to be fit for membership only in the secondary couple, I think, but neither of us had been resigned to that fate for long. The knowledge of my secondariness still stung. I felt that my soul was the soul of a main character, but that my mediocre face and body had begun to deform its growth, the way a constrictive shoe will deform a foot over time or a corset will deform a rib cage. I wondered if Adrienne suffered from this pain as much as I did. Sometimes I still stared into the mirror and hoped that a main character would stare back at me, someone tragic, sleek, and bony, someone whose appearance wouldn't stunt his soul.

"Itgen's," I said. Itgen's was an ice cream parlor an hour's drive from my parents' house, and I had never been there, but its name had the oddness necessary for the game we were playing. I said that an Itgen's sundae required a long spoon, because it was served in a long, old-fashioned glass, not some kind of cup or dish. I had no idea if this was true.

Adrienne nodded. "That's the way a sundae is supposed to be." Barts served sundaes in cardboard bowls, and we agreed that this made their sundaes look like dog food. I said that the whole point of a sundae was its height. Its height, I said, making a wild, loose-wristed gesture, was supposed to intimidate you.

"Totally," she said. The gesture she made when she said "totally" was also loose-wristed and wild. "It's supposed to be so tall that you think you can't finish it and then you do." She grimaced. Out of sheer panic—I still feel bad about it—I put my hand up for a high five. We high-fived. After we had done it, we became quiet and ashamed.

We spent the rest of the orientation group tour of downtown exchanging information about our families—what our parents did for work, what our houses looked like, the ages of our siblings. We went back to my dorm room and I took cans of juice-flavored seltzer from the squat fridge. When I handed her one of the cans, she sipped some of it and reclined in the chair, though it was a desk chair and didn't allow for deep reclining. I remained silent for a while in a standing position, shifting my weight back and forth. We looked at each other. Stooping, I lowered my face toward hers. I could tell, from the way we kissed, that the energy passing through us was shared desperation. Either of us would have kissed almost anybody that day.

We sat on my bed. It made my heart pound to run my hands through her languishing hair, and I felt intense gratitude and admiration, enough to numb the sting of secondariness. It was so good to kiss Adrienne, such an alleviation of sadness and anxiety, that my mind became more lucid than it had been in days, suddenly active, leaping manically from point to point. I wondered if it was the same for her, if she, too, was rehabilitated by the kiss, and was thinking with new clarity about how many of the required courses for an accounting major she should take in her first year, or of the regularity of her period, or of the new season of *Atlanta*. Thoughts were coming at me rapid-fire. Maybe the frat boys and sorority girls made her mad because she was jealous. Did she want to be Queen Cassiopeia of Kappa Gamma? Wasn't that what love was? Taking an ordinary person and turning them into your queen or president? It would be good, I felt, for Adrienne and me to be rulers of our own insignificant mountain. I touched her face with both hands and put my tongue in her mouth. She'd looked regal in the van when she was angry.

She pulled away and tucked strands of hair behind her ears. "Let's slow down," she said. She was flushed, blinking, trying to hide her revulsion. I had gotten carried away. It had happened to me before, with girls. The moment I felt that we had made a breakthrough, that we had found a nonverbal language, that the barriers between us had fallen and we were unified in a single feeling, this turned out to be precisely the moment that I had left my partner behind and slipped away into a private euphoria. It was a lesson I could never remember when I needed to: that the moment of joy in which I believed I had become one with another person was in fact the fall into isolation. She collected her backpack and water bottle. I walked her down the hall to the elevator, for some reason, and the two of us waited side by side at the chrome doors, watching the numbers light up.

A couple of days later, I went home for Labor Day weekend. When I came back, I worked harder at school than I ever had before, sitting on the second floor of the library, where silence was required, highlighting half of the passages in my political science textbook, drinking Diet Coke, and copying and pasting paragraphs from articles into Google Docs that ran thirty pages long. In the aughts, the library had installed a black soundproof booth in the hallway, with the words CELL PHONE ZONE printed in yellow letters on the side. Sitting inside it on the little plastic chair, I delivered an oral presentation aloud.

The second weekend of September, the temperature dropped twenty degrees. There were blotches of red and orange in the trees, the sky spat rain for ten minutes at a time, and stiff winds ruffled the purple flowers in the pots that swayed from the lampposts downtown. The cafeteria workers spoke with satisfaction of the New England weather, and the chairs set out on the sidewalk in front of restaurants fell over. Finally, late Saturday night, I went looking for a party, anything to end my solitude. I followed the sound of music.

At the corner where the two fraternities stood side by side, bands of upperclassmen walked up and down the sidewalk, ten, twelve, fifteen strong. Different kinds of music blared from scattered speakers. Despite the cold, the girls wore shorts or miniskirts, halters or tube tops. They were bright-eyed and unshivering, lit from within. On the porch of Iota Gamma Epsilon, they danced to nineties R&B, took videos of one another, and played cards on a round table, all beneath a canopy of white Christmas lights. There were Christmas lights stapled or glued to three wooden letters propped against the front of their house, standing in the yard, five feet tall, the iota, the gamma, and the epsilon. A clutch of girls posed in front of them as another girl took pictures, and the letters periodically tipped over, forcing them to shove them upright with their shoulders. A blond boy in a white T-shirt walked up and shouted to the girls who were dancing on the porch, asking to come inside the sorority. When they shook their heads no, he screamed, "I'll fuck you up, you cracker-ass bitches." He strutted down the sidewalk with his shoulders thrown back, tossing his great white head like a horse, running his hands through his golden hair. "I'll fuck you up for real, you hear me, you cracker-ass bitches?" He continued to issue the threat at the top of his lungs, over and over, and then he turned the corner down the hill and vanished into one of the smaller houses midway down the slope.

I followed his path down the hill, swerving around the roving groups, until finally they thickened into a mob. Someone shouted above the music, "They're shutting it down, so we're meeting in the parking lot." Police SUVs rolled up and down the street, flashing their blue lights as the crowd flowed around them. "She sent me a video of her pussy and her ass, actually," someone said. To my right, inches away, a boy had lifted his shirt to show his injuries to his friends: "Look at this bad boy here," he said. "And look at this little bad boy, getting his bleed on." Every house had a door flapping open to expose a blue or strobing light, every house had strands of Christmas lights blinking in the windows. "I'm not going to lie," someone said. "I'm not going to front." Cops walked up and down the hill with their hands on their belts. Boys fell and were picked up by the boys on either side of them. A fire truck trundled by, red lights flickering out of sync with the blue lights of the police, and firemen trooped single file into a house on the corner. The scene looked like a protest without the cardboard signs.

A dark-haired girl with sparkling eyeliner reached through the bodies, stumbling, and took my hand. "Hi," she said, grave, and her friends peeled her away. A trio of girls greeted each other, and their screams were bloodcurdling. This crowd would never have been tolerated on the Common, even though the town tolerated all manner of demonstrations, drums, chants, dancing, singing, a hundred spectacles of nonconformity. The Greeks didn't want to be in the right. Their screaming was only a way to say that they excited one another. That was rebellion here. They'd figured it out.

I went into the house to the left of the one with the fire in it, and some of the boys gave me hard looks but nobody stopped me. It was the beginning of the school year, everyone was back together, and the mood was celebratory.

A sheet bearing the yellow-and-black Ferrari stallion logo was hung over the front window. There were spinning green flowers projected on the wall. The music made the floor shake. A girl sat on the shoulders of two boys, pounding punch from a great white bowl. I lapped the floor a couple times, slipped through the dancers without speaking to anyone. People turned and flashed me looks from the safety of their circles. Finally, I leaned against a wall, wearing a bemused expression whose fraudulence I felt as a physical strain in my mouth and eyebrows.

After perhaps thirty seconds there was a tap on my shoulder. It was one of the Deltas—I knew from the letters on his polo shirt—and he held a cup of beer in each hand. "Would you like one of these?" he asked.

The phrasing of the question was oddly formal. He sounded

like a cater-waiter with a tray. His eye contact, too, was strange—unwavering but not challenging.

"Sure," I said. He gave me one of the beers, and we raised our cups and drank. His Delta pledge name was Oprah, he said, and he'd had it for three years now. He still lived in Delta, even though he was a senior and some of the brothers in his class had moved farther from campus. He couldn't imagine leaving, especially now that he had a single. He loved it there.

I thought I knew, then, what was going on: it was pledge season, and he wanted to recruit me. That would explain his manner. The techno on the stereo faded, and a melancholy slow jam began. The wounded singer denounced a lover who'd been untrue. The response from the crowd was immediate: girls who'd been crouched low to the ground unfurled themselves and swayed with their arms in the air; boys didn't sway so much as wobble, flapping their arms mournfully like great endangered birds of prey.

"Don't you love how everyone's so much happier with a sad song on?" asked Oprah. He rubbed one of the buttons on his polo shirt with his thumb. "It makes me feel like the happy songs are just there to help the sad songs kill you."

I asked him what he meant.

He squinted at the ceiling. "This song wouldn't be so good if every song they played was sad. You need most of the music to be everybody-dance-now for the real songs to connect." He made a loose fist and jabbed my solar plexus very gently, and then opened his hand, so that it evoked an explosive projectile connecting with its target, and so that his fingers stroked my chest. It was when he did this, and I laughed, that I first saw flickers of meanness on the faces of the boys on the dance floor.

He asked me questions. This was how he had earned his name, he said, asking questions. He seemed to find my answers, no matter how simple, profound. It made sense that I was from Long Island and had excellent taste in music, he said, because Long Island was next to New York City, where people were sophisticated. It was no wonder, he told me, that I'd been spending all my time in the library, given that I'd grown up so near to a center of learning. He'd never heard of any of my favorite movies, so he wrote down their titles in his phone, as the titles alone, he said, were intriguing. No one had ever offered me so much praise in such a short amount of time. It was possible, I decided, that, while some girls had welcomed my overtures, no girl had ever actively pursued me. This dizzy state was surely the state of being pursued. I felt that it was making me stupid, but in an interesting way. All I had to do was state a fact about myself, and he would labor to find specialness in it. It was like fetch, a game where you stood there feeling imperious and watched the other player work. It was also fetch-like in that I got tired of it before he did.

I was about to excuse myself and leave when one of the boys who'd been on the dance floor only seconds before passed us on the way to the keg and checked each of us with his shoulder, one after the other. He knocked us into the wall, spilling our beers down our shirts. We shouted after him for an explanation, but he only stopped when he reached the keg. He took a fresh cup from the stack and sneered at us as he pumped, his cup tilted 45 degrees to minimize the foam. He was broad in the shoulders, deep in the chest, with the kind of forearms that betokened participation in contact sports. Two other boys standing near the keg watched us and laughed, staring at us with open contempt. Fuck you, I thought, how dare you try to frighten me. My thoughts spiraled off into my usual fantasies of fistfights, retribution. Then it occurred to me that there was something I could do to prove that this subhuman giant had no say in my behavior, that his display of power meant nothing.

In this one quarter mile of town, I realized, this one three-block radius, running off with the boy beside me would be an act of defiance. I pawed the front of his shirt where the beer had soaked through, as if the flesh of my hand were absorbent. I looked up at him—Oprah was a little taller than I was—and ran my thumb over the button he'd rubbed with his own thumb.

"This place is a shithole," I said. "Do you want to go to Delta and show me around?" I danced in place with my eyes closed, briefly. I had never done those two things at the same time, danced and closed my eyes. My voice sounded strange, musical. "Maybe you can show me your room."

He turned and looked at our enemies, tapped his foot, folded his arms. Suddenly, he looked frightened. "Be patient with me," he whispered in my ear. "I've only ever done this with girls." We hurried across the dance floor to the door.

We didn't do some of the things we could have done, because neither of us knew what he was doing. We were both clumsy, that night. And the fact is I've never really fallen for a boy. But in his cramped, overheated bedroom, with the pounding of the bad music outside, and the taste of bad beer in my mouth, and the knowledge that the beer on our clothes was there because someone had wanted us to know we were trash, and the violent idiocy of the chatter on the street, and the lawn below us covered with litter, I liked everything about him. He could do no wrong. I forgot who I was, and what I stood for, and I would have done anything he asked me to do.

# HELL

t was peak foliage, horned red leaves adrift on the duck pond, two-hand touch in the stadium's shadow. It was the time of year for planning new debasements to perform on the pledges during Hell Week, the final test before their initiation. But we were short of ideas. Previous Delta upperclassmen had made their pledges do the elephant walk, in which they were marched through the house each holding the dick of the guy behind him, but we knew that that would no longer fly. It would be filmed on a phone and posted, drawing criticism. Previous upperclassmen had stripped the pledges to their underwear in the back of a van and dropped them off in what was thought to be gang territory in Springfield, but we considered that insensitive to the people who lived there. And the classic procedures—blindfolding the pledges and making them fellate cucumbers or eat bananas out of the toilet—had lost all power to surprise and deceive. The pledges had read online about any torment ever conceived by a pledge educator. The exec board convened at its round plywood table, trying to think who might have some suggestions, when Glines, who was older than the rest of us, having taken time off after junior year to stretch rubber bands over the claws of lobsters and pay down his loans, mentioned a guy we'd never heard of: Michael Poumakis. When Glines was a pledge, Poumakis had been house legend, spoken of in hushed tones by the seniors who remembered him. ROTC, rugby, Honors College, Young Democrats, religious but still brought girls to his room.

When Poumakis graduated, Glines said, he accepted a navy commission. He was Lieutenant Poumakis now; Glines showed us the alumni-database entry on his laptop. He lived in Crystal City, Virginia, a day's drive south.

"If he's an officer outside D.C., guy's probably been through Navy Hell Week," Glines said. "That's SEAL Team Six shit. That's state of the art. That, plus hazing in the navy is probably harsher than anything we would ever come up with. They're preparing you for war."

I was with Glines. A navy guy would know how to take an assortment of pledges and put them through something so strenuous it would bind them into brothers. They wouldn't want to post a picture and get us all in trouble, because they'd be proud they got through it. They'd be proud to be one of us. That was Hell Week's whole point.

We composed the Facebook message as a group, with Glines's laptop on the table between us. We thanked the lieutenant for his service. Regretting that we couldn't provide travel money or accommodations, only Chef Bill's chili, no doubt the same as it had been back in the day, we invited him up for a weekend. *Please consider helping us plan Hell Week this year*, we wrote. *We would be incredibly grateful to draw on the insights you have acquired in your military training as to how to make it an impactful experience for every pledge.*

A response balloon with three dots appeared immediately in the blue window. *I would love to come.*

We had seen full-body shots of him on Instagram, but he looked smaller in real life, stooped by eight hours at the wheel. Since the last picture, he'd grown a beard, and he petted the beard often, the way you would if your beard was new. He dressed like one of those hikers who strive always to be comfy: fleece pants and hoodie, canvas sneakers, moisture-repellent runner's socks, all shades of dun and brown. He petted his upper arms the same way he petted the beard. He was on the cusp of old, about thirty, but he kept his hood up over his head and walked with his hands thrust in his sweatshirt's front pocket, like someone our age.

There was nothing about him that resembled the ads we'd seen for the navy, buzz-cut sailors in starched whites, hands clasped behind their backs on the deck of a carrier, links in the World's Strongest Chain. But his handshake was crushing. He didn't seem to know how much force he applied; for the duration of the exercise his expression remained mild, even kind. All six of us in exec board showed him around the house, though our presence was unnecessary. We followed while Glines led the way, walking backward as he talked. Sometimes he prefaced his remarks with "Moving right along, as you might recall." "Moving right along, as you might recall, these are the couches where you sleep if your roommate has a girl over." "Moving right along, as you might recall, this is the table where the house manager and the president meet every Monday and Thursday." But he spoke in a sarcastic tone, so that the tour was at once serious and self-deprecating. Sometimes he took off his baseball cap and raked his hands through his curls, as if to soothe himself with the feel of his fingernails on his scalp. When we reached the alumni lounge, on the third floor, he sat on the edge of the Ping-Pong table and asked Poumakis what it was like being an officer in the military.

Poumakis spoke in a high, quiet voice. His hood was still up. "The most important thing we do now," he said, "is try to change people's minds. Say, 'Hey, we know it's been hard in your country, we know you've been taught to view us as an enemy, but we want you on our side. We want you to help us create a world where people can vote, and there's basic human rights, and some kind of economic opportunity for everyone. You don't have to be like us, but please, join us.'"

Poumakis touched things: the oars that hung from the study-room wall; the wooden owl mascot; the air rifles racked in the basement; the little sophomore bedrooms, carved from larger bedrooms and crammed with loft beds. When we reached the threshold of the president's room, he touched the chin-up bar in the doorframe, said, "Yup, still here," and lifted off the floor, legs limp and straight.

Glines started to count Poumakis's chin-ups out loud, and then the rest of us had to join in, or Glines's love of Poumakis would be dramatically exposed. It was only fair; we were all a little in love with the soldier in our midst, and it would have been unbrotherly to let Glines stick out, like leaving an injured comrade on the field. As soon as the group counting started—we called out, "Four, five," in chorus, like cadets—Poumakis dropped, bending his knees as he landed.

Glines gave Poumakis a beer from the fridge and guided

him to the black couch on the back porch. He sat beside him and said, "So level with us. How real are the movies about Iraq and Afghanistan and everything? Is that what it's like?" What Glines was trying to ask was, *Have you been in the shit?*

Poumakis wore no particular expression. There was a slot in his beard that opened and shut. "I thought *Zero Dark Thirty* was okay," he said. "They showed it was a lot of people coordinating instead of one person doing everything. But they never showed anyone being funny, except for Chris Pratt at the end. I liked Chris Pratt because he's funny. Still, when they were working in the office in Pakistan, none of them were ever funny. They were always serious. They were never like, 'Okay, it's eleven o'clock, who wants doughnuts?'"

The sun had set over the decrepit unaffiliated green Victorian that backed up against our yard. Rumor had it that it was all high school dropouts living off a grandma they kept in the attic. Their living room lights came on, and then music, a dance remix of a song about being sad in the summertime.

"But was it typical," Glines asked, "of how people go undercover and find terrorists, and take them?"

What Glines meant was, *Have you gone undercover? Have you killed?*

Poumakis picked at the label on his beer. "I wouldn't say typical," he said.

"I want you to know," said Glines, "that we're your brothers. Whatever you say never leaves the porch."

"I can neither confirm nor deny," said Poumakis. He inhaled through his nose. He might have resumed talking for no other reason but to fill the silence.

"The first mode of cover they teach in training," he said, "the one that's most typical in the field, is called You Me Same Same. I don't know where the name came from. I think it's probably African or Caribbean, but some people think it's from this novel from the eighties. There's this Vietnamese girl, and she's really hot and she's Vietcong, and they've got her captured. She's scared they're going to rape her. And she points to a Native American GI, and points to her face, and goes, 'You, me, same, same.'"

We all looked at one another and pointed. "You, me, same, same," we said, making come-hither faces. Poumakis looked amused. We waited, rapt.

"Wherever the name comes from," he said, "the idea with You Me Same Same is, you create a cover identity that makes the target feel like the two of you are similar. You become a person who reminds the target of him- or herself. The first objective is to research the target's tastes, passions, and interests, and familiarize yourself as best you can. The second is to persuade the target that you're like him, only a little more confident, a little nicer. Which is all he's ever wanted from a partner or a friend. It's like dating."

Glines was grinning like a fool, like an innocent. He was grinning like a guy who's just asked his high school sweetheart to marry him at Fenway. I felt it, too. I felt like my life had been a dream in which nothing mattered, and finally I was waking up into a world that was real, a world where people fought. It was really true that I was alive.

"So who would do that?" Glines asked Poumakis, his voice shaky with joy. "The CIA?"

"Usually more conventional military granted temporary status as intelligence," Poumakis said. "CIA guys tend to take advantage of how everything kind of loosened up after 9/11 by farming out the fieldwork to us. The CIA is good at intelligence gathering, intelligence analysis, and planning paramilitary operations. But not when it comes to doing the actual ops. We're better at fieldwork than they are. It's there in the statistics. So what are we going to do? Tell them, like, 'Fuck off, I signed up for the navy?'"

We were all nodding as if we related. We needed some way to express our exhilaration, and nodding was the available vehicle. But of the six of us, only Glines was so high on Poumakis that he could overcome his shyness and ask him what we all wanted to ask.

"You've done that?" asked Glines. "Ops? You Me Same Same?"

Poumakis took a Juul from a pocket of his sweatpants and puffed. "My first target was in Sudan. He loved the Canadian Brass. He was obsessed with these two albums, *Bach: The Art of Fugue* and *Live in Germany*. I bought them on old-school CD from a University of Khartoum student. I sat in my apartment and listened to them for hours.

"I bought a new wallet, which was tan, not black like my real one. I bought a Paul Smith suit with subtle stripes and vintage Nike sneakers because my research indicated my target thought those things were cool. I rented an apartment and got the kind of furniture he would've bought. It's something they teach you to do, getting the furniture, so that you feel like a different person. And you need everything you can get that will make you feel like it will work, because you're not an actor, and here you are acting. When I hung out with this guy—we went to this café on Nile Street—I was worried I would spill my glass of tea down my striped suit because I was faking. I thought faking would be stressful. But then this weird thing happened. I found out I was more relaxed in cover than when I wasn't in cover. It was easier than being not in cover, kind of."

"That's because you're a natural," said Glines.

"In cover, daily life wasn't that stressful at all," Poumakis continued. "Sometimes I liked pretending to enjoy horn quintets with a target more than I liked talking about, say, Arcade Fire, my actual favorite band, with a person I actually liked. It was just easier. The awkwardness of trying to be real with someone went away. You didn't have to try to be real. I'm pretty sure I have mild PTSD, and I get this depression that comes for a little while and then goes. That didn't happen when I was in cover. It was like being drunk."

Glines gave himself a neck rub. "If it's like being drunk, sign me up," he said. "I'm going to Sudan."

Next door, someone threw a Frisbee into a tree. The leaves sprayed water into the air as the disc flew through them.

"It's great to have you here," I said to Poumakis. "But besides just getting to grill you about all the badass stuff you've done, we were kind of hoping you could give us some advice. You've done Navy Hell Week, probably, right? Tell us the tricks you learned. How do you make things shitty for a bunch of pledges?"

Poumakis vaped again. "Navy Hell Week," he said, "is, you're swimming in the ocean on four hours of sleep catching hypothermia and there are drill instructors with megaphones telling you it's cool if you want to quit and go have coffee and muffins. They're shouting at you about how there's no dishonor in quitting, go set yourself free. They want seventy-five percent of you to quit, they expect you to bail. You're not trying to make these pledges quit. Because if seventy-five percent of your pledges quit, you don't have a fraternity." We conceded that this was the case. "You want to make things shitty for a guy? Lock him up and leave him alone."

"Have you done that?" Glines asked. "In the field?"

"I've done interrogations," he said. "And the weird thing is, people can't stand it when you leave them by themselves. They bang on the walls until they elicit a response. Or they pretend to be sick until they elicit a response."

Glines rubbed his knees. "You put them in a box or something?"

Poumakis shook his head. "With this guy in Sudan, I put him in a room for a week. Not a box. A clean, plain room with food and water. Then I'd bring him out and You Me Same Same with him. He was always up for small talk, even to me. The next day, I offered him a sparkling water. We went for a walk, under guard. The day after that, I said, 'Come on up to our quote-unquote kitchen, we've got some cabbage, some yogurt, some eggs, some fruit. Let's see if we can slap together a real meal, because neither of us wants to be here but while we're stuck here, might as well, right?'

"The next thing you know, he's like, 'It's better than the food at camp.' And later, he's like, 'You think your rifles are shit? You should see the shit rifles we have.' Gradually, he gave me more and more of what I was after. He wanted to keep it going. He wanted company.

"He had to know what I was doing, but he went into denial about it. That's how much he hated being by himself. That's how badly he wanted some You Me Same Same. Can you imagine how he felt, when I put him back in his room and he thought about the information he'd given me in exchange for a little bit of bullshitting? It must have been torture for him. I tortured the guy, in a way, is I guess what I'm saying."

"He sounds like a pussy, though," said Glines. "It wouldn't have been torture for a guy with balls. It would have been dinner."

There was something about this last word, the way it hung in the air. For the first time, Poumakis seemed annoyed. The lower half of his face disappeared into his hood. Instead of stroking his beard, or his fleeces, his hands lay still on his knees.

"If you want to make Hell Week bad for a pledge," he said, "I'll tell you what you do. You bring him into this house, and you lock him in one of the bedrooms. Throw in some milk and bananas, throw in some water. Give him a bedroom that has a bathroom, with a toothbrush, a shower. Take away his phone, don't let anyone visit. For the first few days, he'll beg and plead with you. He'll say, 'Please, take me out of here.' Then he'll stop, and for the next few days, he'll cuss you out. He'll say, 'Fuck you, I don't care what you do to me anymore. I hate you. Don't come near me.'"

Poumakis drew the hood back from his face. He swiped at his cheeks as if there were a mosquito trying to bite him.

His eyes were bright and brown and he raised his scant eyebrows, settling into his lecture. The music was different now, a song about going out and having a good time. As the singer discussed a night in the club, the dance floor, the VIP, the labels on his clothing, a kid with a shaved head and full-sleeve tattoos slouched out of the house and got on a bike that was too small for him. We watched him ride a circle around his yard, one hand on the left handlebar, the other hanging at his side.

"When the week is over, you let him out of the room. But don't let him out of the house. Let him take a walk down the hall. Let him look out the window. Let him walk up and down the stairs. Invite him to dinner."

Glines looked at the grass. He had his head down and was fiddling with the brim of his cap. Without meaning to, I shook my head at Poumakis. I didn't want him to keep going, because I didn't want Glines to be further shamed. But Poumakis wasn't looking at me. He was looking out over the yard, tugging his beard into a triangle. Just as his face had remained gentle during his brutal handshakes, so did it remain gentle during his humiliation of Glines.

"Offer him the best food you have," he said. "Chef Bill's chili. Pour him a nice cold beer. Gather round the table, and say, 'Welcome, brother. Pull up a chair. We're the ones who did that to you, and we're in charge of everything. No need to be shy. Please, join us.'"

# SAFE
# SPACES

laire's roommates threw her out on November third, for falling behind on rent and hogging the Xbox. During the next three weeks, she lived in other people's houses. She missed the Xbox, but couch surfing was like a game. She had to not smell like coke-sweat or wipe her nose all the time in front of her hosts, and she had to figure out the magic words that would make them let her stay. At her aunt's house, she praised a samovar. Ding-ding, *x 3 nights*. At her friend Abby's mom's house, she praised a sword, and held it, at the invitation of its owner, Abby's mom's boyfriend, a former military school instructor, and slipped it back into its wall-mounted case, resting the blade and pommel in the felt slot. Ding-ding, *x 2 nights*. In Abby's mom's boyfriend's gap-toothed son's house, she praised the smell of cows as the first snow of winter fell through sunlight and country music played on the stereo. Doo-da-la-ding, *x 4 nights*. In Abby's bed, she and Abby had sex, and Abby asked, "Why won't you look at me?" but she couldn't make prolonged eye contact with Abby: *x 1 night*. In Abby's mom's boyfriend's gap-toothed son's ex-wife's house, she told the ex-wife about the gap-toothed son's girlfriend, shared two lines with the ex-wife, watched her clean the living room, and held the ladder so she could wipe down the candle-flame-shaped light bulbs in the chandelier: *x 2 nights*. The cocaine made it even more like a game because when she found a place to sleep she didn't really sleep. She dozed two or three hours and bolted upright. She wanted to stay in bed forever and also to get up and break things, but she never slept all day or broke anything, just lay there half awake until the sun rose, her alarm went off, and it was time to go to work. By mid-November, she was a master of the whole routine, she felt no fear. But then pilgrim hats and turkeys appeared in the windows of the stores, and the game froze.

The week of Thanksgiving there were no more places to crash, because everybody she knew was either traveling or hosting. Scottish Inns, the Rodeway, and the Granby Motel were all full. Even no-pics Puffton Village bedrooms on Craigslist were priced to take advantage of the holiday. Abby, who always let her stay in a pinch, had been turned against her by puritanical friends who considered her a bad influence. Claire was the only person Abby had ever done coke with, and Abby's nerd mafia of beautiful, frightening Jewish and Armenian girls had freaked out about how Abby kept showing up at the bio lab spilling coffee and grinding her jaw.

Tuesday morning, Claire left one of the last cheap Airbnbs downtown and worked a six-hour shift at Dunkin', where the tiles in the bathroom were large and brown, with wet tracks left by boots and sneakers. After work, she walked to the public library. The bathroom off the children's zone had a lockable door and a diaper-changing station, where you could cut a line vigorously without having to worry about some of it spilling off the side, which could happen when you used the top of a toilet-seat-cover dispenser. The walls were pale orange, with a framed drawing of nineteenth-century animals absorbed in books. The changing station's yellow foldout surface was shaped like a baby, with stubby arms and legs. A private bathroom, like this one, was a safe place for flatulence. That was one of her physical reactions to coke, and it always started psychosomatically, after she'd poured some coke onto a surface but before she'd actually snorted any. She fretted a rail from a clump with her debit card, dead center of the baby, and when she did the rail it burned. Her right nasal passage felt exactly as if it had been stung by a bee.

She liked the corroded upper cone of her right nasal passage. It was trusty, like an old truck. And besides, this month, for some reason, her left nasal passage was ornery and sensitive. While she waited for the numbness, it was hard not to blow her nose, because when she was feeling the level of discomfort she now felt, she wanted to expel some mucus into a tissue and glimpse with her own eyes some sign of what the medical situation might be, to know for a fact that there was no crust, glob, or other blood event up there where the cone gave onto tunnels she couldn't see. But if she blew her nose before her right nasal passage went numb, the pain would get worse.

Here was the numbness. She blew her nose and checked the Kleenex: the usual red spiders bathed in clear froth. Grateful that there was no bad news in the Kleenex, she did the trampoline. "The trampoline" was Abby's term for the repetitive motion Claire made when she was happy: while doing knee bends, she clapped her fingers against her thumbs as if playing castanets. Claire was one-eighth autistic, by her own estimate, the way some people were one-eighth black or one-eighth straight, and whatever eighth you were, that shit was going to come out in how you moved when you were pleased with yourself. She'd done the trampoline all her life—and she wasn't the only one, she'd seen Scripps National Spelling Bee finalists do it on YouTube—but coke could bring it on. She bounced as she cleaned the baby-shaped table with her finger, rubbing her gums with the leftovers her finger collected. Then a woman with a baby knocked and said hello—she could hear the baby screaming on the other side of the door—and she had to leave the bathroom.

She abandoned the library, which, at this time in the afternoon, was liable to fill with kids any minute, and walked out into the damp air, her sneakers squishing on the slush-covered flagstone path that bisected the library's front lawn. The late-November wind blew into her face, and the freezing feeling in her raw, unnumbed left nostril reminded her of a frigid morning last week, when Abby had walked outside, high, with her hair wet, and studied it, amazed, totally stupid, as it iced over and stiffened. What a cum laude moment. She had a brain, Abby—she was one of the top bio majors in the Honors College—and she needed somebody like Claire, somebody more grounded in the real world. But it wasn't just Abby's science-genius retardation Claire loved, it was her head shaped like Tweety Bird's, her sandy hair combed back from her pale forehead, the thin blue veins on her temples, the acne around her mouth. Her nose was even curved like Tweety Bird's beak. That one time Abby had let Claire go down on her for fifteen minutes, that was the closest Claire had ever come to finding a grand purpose in life, forcing Abby's face to go 100 percent brainless. And fate was conspiring to bring them together because Thanksgiving had made Claire need to stay with Abby like never before. It was urgent now that Abby ignore her bitter, unexciting friends and acknowledge the insane and undeniable vibe that she had with Claire. Claire was in the midst of an all-important revelation: Abby was the love of her life. She would present herself to Abby, bedraggled but proud, and the vibe would fill the air and Abby would be moved and turned on and take her in, to stay in her off-campus apartment, eventually for good. And Claire would make a speech at their wedding about how she knew how strong Abby was, how generous, when, during a hard time in her life, Abby had seen through the superficialities and put up with her. She would gaze across the crowd, point to Abby's mother, and say, *You have raised a daughter who is brave and good*, and Abby's mother would cry.

Best to approach Abby in person about needing a place to stay, because one way to get Abby to hang out, historically, was to pour some cocaine on a surface and offer her a casually improvised tube, such as a rolled bill, without actually verbally introducing the subject of cocaine. She looked on her phone to see if Abby had left any clues as to whether she was going anywhere or doing anything specific today. And in fact, as it happened, Abby'd tweeted that she was feeling fucked up and depressed about the election, and that she hoped to see a lot of people at the Pride Alliance meeting at five.

The Pride Alliance meeting was happening at the Stonewall Center, in Crampton Hall. It was just for students, but Claire was a former student, and student-aged. Claire killed a couple hours at Share Coffee, drinking a hot chocolate and then a mocha, doing a follow-up bump in a stall, playing *Warcraft* on her laptop in the corner, trying to be quiet on the headset, still getting looks, and then bent her steps toward the university she'd once attended, the wide, rectangular towers with their fronts and backs vested in red brick, their sides bare concrete. Why had Massachusetts made its biggest college look like public housing? Wasn't a college the opposite of a public-housing project?

It wasn't really winter yet. Still, a tree dripped a finger of cold water down her neck as she walked beneath it, following the bike path to campus. To stay in the high, she thought of the Xbox games she missed. She liked the *Zelda* rip-offs, like *Darksiders*, because they moved fast and because she felt bad for the heroes and heroines. They were always in a kill-or-be-killed situation, and you saw their backs, their little hardworking buttocks, the soles of their boots as they ran.

She reached the Southwest Residential Area, where she swerved to avoid the stubborn patches of ice on the salted paths. It was the weirdest thing about the university: anyone could just saunter on in. She'd been to Boston, to visit a friend who'd run away there, and at Harvard it was the same deal. You could cross Harvard Yard, lie on it. How did anyone at Harvard know it wasn't full of people like her? How did the students feel safe with the gates open, and no one asking what she was doing, why she was there?

Crampton Hall was a long, four-story brick rectangle with yellow iron lozenges set in the railings as decorative accents. Claire walked into the Stonewall Center's classroom precisely on time. A rainbow flag was pinned to the wall, and beside it hung a photo of gender nonconforming people marching six abreast down a street in New York. The chairs were fitted with small desks and wheels. Students sat at them and propelled them into a circle by walking their legs across the brick-colored carpet, or by pushing against the carpet with both legs at the same time, a kind of rowing. The rowers got into it, rolled their hips, made the desks glide.

Abby hurried in late, sandwiched between two of her most narrow-minded and virginal-seeming friends. They were two of the friends Abby had named when she gave Claire a list of people who considered Claire bad news, counting them off on her fingers. They were looking directly at Claire with no expression, like that was supposed to frighten her or something. Claire admitted to herself that she found even the most awkward of the brains who constituted Abby's social circle attractive. These two were both strong-looking, with thick legs and wide torsos, outfitted in pastel-colored winter clothing, like the posse that follows around a rapper. They were both wearing headbands! She laughed and crossed her legs, because she, Claire, was such a pointed contrast, merry and lithe, her eyes probably twinkling. She tried to twinkle them at Abby. Abby was wearing a gray hoodie that said PIONEER VALLEY LIGHT OPERA on it. She was pretending that Claire wasn't there, that her friends weren't gazing at Claire with consternation. She was sitting up straight with her hands on her knees and her chin in the air. To avoid meeting Claire's eyes, she was studying the drop ceiling. The other students, oblivious to the war Claire was waging against Abby's bodyguards, slumped in their chairs and clasped their hands behind their heads. Others sat cross-legged with their arms folded. One of the bodyguards stopped looking at Claire long enough to rub lotion on her hands. The other took a picture of the wind-whipped trees outside, pretending the trees were pretty, making awed sounds.

Elizabeth from Saugus started the meeting by saying that this was the first place she'd felt comfortable crying since Trump was elected a few weeks ago. She put her face in her hands and sobbed. Daniela from Mattapan said that the joke among her friends was to bet on which one of them was going to get deported. Josh from Sterling had been called a faggot by kids on his street for the first time. Frank from East Longmeadow read aloud a Snapchat message from a kid he'd known in high school that said, *Now you will have to stop cocksucking or die.* Jasmine from Chicopee said that her friend's little brother had chased a Muslim girl. Paula from Lee said that it was important, in this nightmare situation, for their community to stick together, no matter what.

Claire tapped the side of her nose at Abby, which meant, *Do you want to meet me in the bathroom?* At first, Abby didn't react. But then Claire did it again. She turned one nostril toward Abby and tapped it, and then she turned the other nostril toward Abby and tapped it, like the cancan except with nostrils. Abby started to break. She put her hands over her mouth. Then her hands parted, and she smiled in the way Claire loved most, like a scientist smiling at a bizarre creature she'd discovered under a microscope. Claire jerked her head toward the door. The bodyguards looked at Claire with drawn, furious faces.

But Abby probably wasn't going to ditch the meeting while everyone was getting emotional, Claire knew. She was too polite. That was part of Abby's charm, the way she needed to be rescued from her own nature.

Vanessa from Easthampton said she'd thought this was a safe country to be in, but now? She frowned and kneaded her eyelids with her thumbs. "What are we going to do?" she asked.

Josh from Sterling said that he didn't know, maybe they should have a dance party. This was not a serious suggestion. But then Frank played a song on his phone. It went: *I live in the hood / Where fuckboi don't come.* Frank and Josh started to dance. One by one, the students rose from their chairs and joined them. Eventually, the bodyguards stood and danced with Abby, exercising their limbs without pattern or rhythm. But even the students who could follow the beat, like Abby, danced in quotes. Did students dance in quotes the world over? Claire hadn't when she was a student here, she didn't think. At any rate, Claire saw that she was an infinitely better dancer than everyone else at the meeting, so she danced. She danced like someone having sex with a little person, and some of the students copied her, dancing like people having sex with little people. She danced like someone being tased, and some of the students danced like people being tased. She danced like someone who'd drunk poison, staggering in place, and some of the students danced like people who'd drunk poison, and, finally, doing the poisoned dance, some of them stopped dancing in quotes and dance danced.

As the song faded, Claire dashed between the bodyguards and put her mouth to Abby's ear. The weather had made Abby's hair smell like the rabbit Claire had owned in elementary school. "What are you doing tonight?" Claire asked.

"I'm worried about you," Abby said.

Claire nodded. She waited for her answer.

Abby whispered in her ear, so that the bodyguards wouldn't hear. "I'm going to the Campus Progressives thing at seven."

At the Labor Center, where Campus Progressives convened, there were chairs with small desks attached to them, as in Crampton Hall, but here the chairs had no wheels. In order to arrange them into a circle, people lifted them into the air. There were wood-laminate bookshelves with cranks on their sides, and if you turned the cranks they trundled in one direction or the other, depending on which way you turned. Claire had done a tiny bump off an upright piano in one of the practice rooms in the Fine Arts Center, and now it was funny to crash one shelf into its neighbor, draw it back, and crash it again, in slow motion. After she did this a couple times, she noticed a sheet of paper taped to the door on which someone had written, in capitals: CAMPUS PROGRESSIVES, PLEASE DOWNLOAD SIGNAL TO RECEIVE COMMUNICATIONS. THIS MEANS YOU! Abby entered without her entourage shortly after Claire had downloaded Signal. Claire wanted to lift her into the air, like a desk. She patted the chair next to hers, and Abby sat in it.

"Hey," said Abby, and waved, as if Claire were a fellow progressive who wasn't in love with her and trying to sleep in her house.

"Have you downloaded Signal on your phone yet?" Claire asked.

Abby nodded. "Yeah, it's got a pretty good reputation for privacy. It's recommended by Edward Snowden."

*Let's go to your apartment,* Claire signaled Abby.

Abby didn't acknowledge Claire's proposal in real life. In reply, she signaled back an emoji of a video-game controller.

*Not just to play Xbox I promise I actually want to hang out with you,* Claire signaled, and sent Abby a list of things she wanted to do with her in bed. Signal, a tool of dissidents, its screen trimmed in periwinkle blue, made sexting feel life-affirming and brave, like masturbating on the toilet at work.

Abby coughed. "It looks like they're getting started," she said aloud.

Sure enough, the other people in the circle had begun to introduce themselves. Scott said he'd predicted it would just be the diehards tonight, since everyone was about to go home and eat cranberry sauce, and that he was personally wowed by the turnout. John said it was time to strike while the iron was hot, he'd never seen people so pumped, even though it was a nightmare come to life.

*Abby,* Claire signaled, *if I go to the bathroom now, and you follow me there after a second, no one will think it's weird. We'll just get a little bit high. It helps you concentrate when people are being boring.*

Jasmine said that if ever there was a time for activism, it was now.

*Abby.* Claire tapped rapidly with her thumbs, her phone on her desk. *Don't you think maybe if you just do a couple of small lines, then you are going to be an excellent activist for the rest of the meeting and beyond?* Abby had her phone on her lap, but she was still reading Claire's messages, peering down at the screen of the Signal app when a message lit it up.

Henry raised his hand. "I'm sorry to speak out of turn," he said. "But I think it's time to start talking about what we could do just at a regional level. What one could do is interesting, regionally, because the university is half the population of the town, nine months of the year, and there's a lot of momentum behind the idea of sanctuary areas. Could we, in effect, have a local secession? I don't mean the use of force. Just, what if we focus our activism on local races? We could make this one town where we control the police, the schools. I mean it's funny, but could a collection of people with our views actually take over? Say, this is one place, in this shit show of a country we're living in, where hope is still alive? I mean, what could we do if we had the entire town council, or whatever it is? Maybe we could make it so that the cops were actually on our side here."

Most of Henry's head was shaved, but there was a brain of hair on top. He was small, rosy-cheeked, pockmarked. His jeans fit as if dryer fresh. After he'd spoken, he folded his arms and looked at his shoes. Claire applauded, followed by almost every other person in the room, even as some shook their heads.

Claire signaled Abby, *That guy is kind of cool. Wrong word? Actually moron?*

A number of people spoke at once about what it might look like if progressives established local rule. In Claire's attempt to catch everything, she found it hard to follow any given thread to its end. This was the problem with cocaine. She heard: *state cops, horticulture, revolutionary, education major.* They had so many ideas about how the future version of the town could be that it was as if they were already living in it.

"We need an antihegemonic song," a guy said.

"Are there even antihegemonic songs?" another guy asked.

"'Everybody Wants to Rule the World,'" Abby said.

Oh, fuck, Abby! Fucking Abby! She was so funny, and now Claire was fairly sure she knew what *antihegemonic* meant. To have that voice in your head for the rest of your life!

There was a tap on her shoulder. It was Jasmine. Her face was close to Claire's, and she was making her expression gentle. "I'm so sorry to have to ask this," she said. "But, since we have security rules here, to protect people's privacy, and you're texting a lot while people are talking, which is actually making some people uncomfortable, and I've never seen you here before today, I have to ask you: Are you part of the university community?"

Claire laughed. She turned to Abby and said, with her face, *Can you believe this shit?* But Abby was quiet. She hung her head and blinked at the fake-wood plane of her desk. The other people in the room were still talking about the practicalities of a de facto secession.

It was kind of adorable that they thought she might expose their plan to turn Amherst into a country. If she wanted to, she could say that she'd once been a student here, but that she'd lost her financial aid because she'd failed some classes. That would make Jasmine shut up. But when she imagined saying that—in essence pleading, *Don't be mean to me, I'm so fucked, you're so privileged, please let me be a part of your awesome revolution*—she felt what was left of her buzz turn into hatred. How was she supposed to seduce Abby if Abby had to watch her roll over on her back and show her throat?

"Sorry," Claire said. "I didn't mean to make anybody uncomfortable." She picked up her backpack and walked out, wiping her nose so as not to have to look at anyone. It was possible, she thought, that Abby was watching her with longing and admiration. But if Abby was looking at the wall, embarrassed to be associated with her, she didn't want to know.

It was now truly cold outside. The streetlight by the duck pond lit a fringe of ice and within the fringe a lip of semisolid white. Another problem with coke was the stretch when you wanted to die. Her backpack was heavy. It was purple because she'd picked it out in tenth grade, and the main zipper had lost its tab so that now there was only a stud that had to be coaxed along the teeth. She slouched into the wind, her hands in her jacket pockets. The wind plucked a goose feather from a tear in the jacket's arm, around the edges of the X of tape, and the feather twirled into the dark. Another feather nosed its way out of the tear, bit by bit, until the upper half of the feather's spine was exposed and whipped against the jacket's skin, and finally this feather, too, broke free and twirled away. It was time to call home. Or no, not yet.

Because here was an enormous crèche. The house was a symmetrical wooden colonial, three stories tall, with a columned facade that shed chips of brown paint. Letters from the ancient world were nailed to the portico's triangular face. Three boys conferred between the columns, beneath the letters, gazing down at one of their phones, the phone candling their faces. All the windows were lit, and silhouettes lurched across the golden squares. She had never sold coke at this particular fraternity, but she'd had some luck with a couple of others. What she really needed was a place to crash. That just wasn't the way to put it, at first.

On her way up the steps of the portico, she asked the boys if they might know anybody who might want some cocaine.

The rightmost of the three boys, a towering athlete, laughed and clapped, his clapping muted by mittens. "Hello, random badass," he said.

"Damn," agreed the pudgy guy in the middle, who held the phone and wore a runner's headband on his shaved head. "You are an honest person," he told Claire.

"I'm serious, though," she said.

The boys looked at each other. The leftmost, whose curly hair sprung from beneath a beanie, stroked his chin. "If I were you," he said, "I'd see if there's this one kid in front of the PlayStation. Little guy. He looks like . . ." He struggled for words.

"Oh yeah," said the athlete. "Kyle. He's cool. His hair is cool. And this time of night, he'll be at the PlayStation, most def. This is what he does." With great precision, without cruelty, he impersonated the flailing of a gamer, mashing the buttons of an invisible controller, bending his torso all the way to one side, whipping it all the way to the other, and back to the middle again.

"That's actually really helpful," she said. "Thanks."

They parted to make way for her, and she walked between

them, across the porch and through the front door, which was propped open with an Oakley sunglasses case. She made her way through a dark, narrow foyer, upsetting a snow shovel before she passed into the living room, big, bright, and medieval, with high ceilings.

The walls were covered in woolly banners: the disembodied head of the Patriots, with its tricorn hat; the golden wheel of the Bruins; the leprechaun of the Celtics, twirling a ball and leaning on his knobby spike of a cane. There were two more bros drinking beer on a couch in the corner, listening to Madlib, and, as promised, a small, wiry bro playing PS4, cross-legged before a screen. Claire sat on her knees beside him and learned that he was in fact Kyle. His Delta pledge name, he added, was Wagon Wheel, because he was good at singing "Wagon Wheel." Right now, Claire noticed, he was showing a fair amount of skill at *Bloodborne*.

"I can tell you've done this nightmare before," she said.

He nodded.

"You should try it on coke." She shrugged. "I've got some. Have you ever done it?"

He laughed and shook his head. "The thing is," he said, "I'm already on Adderall, so I'm worried it would just be—" He made a soft, explosive sound and continued playing. She sensed he was neural kin; there was the static, preoccupied expression, the rocking of the torso, the hiding eyes, the small body, the hair that stood in bunches. He was cokie, metabolically.

"You'd like it," she said. "I can tell."

"Are you a pusher?" he asked, as he worked the controller. "I thought that was something that only existed in movies."

"I sell it," she said. "I don't push it on anybody." Coke was more fun than Adderall, she explained. A gram would be well worth his while, an investment. Anytime he wanted to offer people just a little bit and get the party started, he could. A hundred bucks was a reasonable price. It was not a lot of money for trying something that could be a good drug for him, a fun drug but also a study drug for when his prescription wasn't enough.

The Hunter, operated by Wagon Wheel, was fighting the Wet Nurse in her lair.

"Do you always make the Hunter male?" she asked.

"I go back and forth," he said.

"Me too."

"Do you go to school?"

She shook her head.

"I thought so," he said. "I was like, why would she be selling the shit out of something like that if she was in school, with everything taken care of?"

She was starting to find him a little annoying. *Where are you?* she signaled Abby. There was no answer. *I'm sorry I fucked up,* she continued. *I know I was bad today.*

After a few seconds, there were dots by Abby's name. Then: *Please stop contacting Abby. She doesn't want to be in touch with you right now.*

She wondered which one of them it was. Jasmine? The bodyguards? Never mind, she thought, no point dwelling on it. She felt ill, but there was shit she had to do: get paid, get nights. Fuck those people and the bubble they lived in.

"Hey," said Wagon Wheel. He paused the game and squinted at her. "Are you okay? You were looking at your phone and you just kind of . . ." He pantomimed a slump. "Oh, shit," he said, when he noticed she'd begun to cry. "What's wrong?"

It was quiet with the game paused. "I like this girl and she doesn't like me back," she said. She gestured toward the controller, to indicate that he should resume playing.

"Sorry," he said. "I've been there, with girls. It always feels like they're killing you. And then they go spread their legs for some confident asshole." He unpaused the game and continued the fight. She sat and cried and watched him run in circles to escape a spell.

"Hey, could I play for a second?" she asked. "I won't fuck it up, I swear. I'm pretty good."

He gave her the controller. She dried her eyes with her knuckles and wiped her nose with the heel of her hand. And everything narrowed to the keep in which the Wet Nurse lived. The Hunter's health was diminished, but Wagon Wheel had neglected to use his arrows; the quiver was full. His problem was that he couldn't figure out how to evade the Wet Nurse's swords for long enough to load the bow. Claire knew how to do it on the run.

As she played, Wagon Wheel made choking sounds. He summoned the two boys on the couch and the three of them stood behind her to watch. She hummed along with the Wet Nurse's lullaby, a waltz played on a harpsichord with loose keys. This was something she often did when she fought a boss, hummed along with the boss's special soundtrack. She paused the game to take off her sneakers, and after a minute she found a groove. Over and over, she dodged a swipe of the claws, nocked an arrow, and retreated with a parting shot. Soon the

Wet Nurse flagged. Claire ducked behind her and swung the poisoned scythe. When the Wet Nurse's final spell expired, Claire finished her off with Molotov cocktails, and her death wails were drowned by the Deltas' cheers.

She tossed the controller to the floor, to let Wagon Wheel decide what the Hunter should do next. It had been a while since she'd fucked with *Bloodborne*, and it had felt good to kill the Wet Nurse again. The boys were scratching their necks and asking for information: How did she know when to switch to the scythe? How did she jump backward at a diagonal, and how did she know when she was out of range of a spell? But Claire didn't feel like explaining it all. She was so tired. It had been over a month since she'd had a good night's sleep. It had been a long time since she'd cried. The last bump had been the tiny one in the practice room before Campus Progressives, and that was okay. She was sad in a way that didn't call for cocaine, that called for soft surfaces rather than hard. The rug on which she sat was not luxuriant. Its pile was not high. It smelled of beer and ash. That, too, was okay. She stretched to her full length, and the boys shuffled out of her way. They had stopped waiting for her to answer their questions and were theorizing about her technique. Her puffy coat made a decent cushion. It released a feather when she rolled her head, and she watched the feather's slow descent. Still humming the Wet Nurse's lullaby, she spread her fingers to work the gamer's cramp from her hands. With the Deltas standing over her, murmuring among themselves, and the game's music swelling and victorious, she closed her eyes and dreamed.

## ACKNOWLEDGMENTS

The author is grateful to Mitzi Angel, Claudia Ballard, Lorin and Sadie Stein, Molly Walls, Gemma Sieff, Christine Smallwood, Greg Jackson, Caleb Crain, Rachel B. Glaser, Robin Wasserman, Nicole Rudick, Amie Barrodale, Clancy Martin, Rob Spillman, Rafil Kroll-Zaidi, Anthony Vinci, Rodrigo Corral, Jason Fulford, Laird Gallagher, Mark Jude Poirier, Ben Neihart, Lexy Benaim, Allan Gurganus, Annie Baker, Linda Baker, Conn Nugent, Yaddo, MacDowell, Ucross, the staff and board of *The Paris Review*, and the Greeks and non-Greeks who shared their stories.

A NOTE ABOUT THE AUTHOR

Benjamin Nugent is the winner of *The Paris Review*'s 2019 Terry Southern Prize. His stories have been published in *The Best American Short Stories*, *The Best American Nonrequired Reading*, and *The Unprofessionals: New American Writing from The Paris Review*. Nugent has also written for *n+1*, *The New York Times Magazine*, *The New York Times Book Review*, and *Time*.